Daybreak
A Howl in the Night Book Four

Courtney Rene

Chapter One

The sun was just beginning to crest over the horizon. It tossed reds, oranges and even a smattering of yellows high into the sky where it tried to push back the darkness of the night. The wet air began to settle in droplets on the dark green grass, where it then soaked into my skin and clothes. Sadly, it didn't cool my over-warm body; instead it seemed to make me feel even more sticky and hot. The day, once it fully arrived, would be another scorcher, and if the dew around me was any indication, it would be just as humid as the day before.

"What are you doing out here?"

I turned just my head away from the glorious dawn and focused my eyes on the tall, dark, and half-clothed man standing right up next to where I lay in the damp grass. My eyes traveled from his bare feet, up his long and muscled torso, to his face, that was shadowed just enough I couldn't read his expression. "Derek," I said.

"Yeah, it's me. What are you doing?"

"I couldn't sleep. I came out to watch the sunrise."

"By yourself?"

As the answer was evidently yes, I didn't respond. Instead, I took a deep breath and sat up.

I heard him sigh. He dropped down to sit next to me. He pressed against my arm. His skin was warm, and I leaned into it. Not that I was cold, as it was hot as hell, but it was comforting and warm and I wanted to soak it up. "Okay, how about, why are you out here at the buttcrack of dawn, by yourself?"

I huffed a quiet laugh at his press of humor. "I couldn't sleep. All I kept thinking about was the boy. I feel…guilty over the whole thing. What will happen to him, Derek?"

He wrapped his arms around me and pulled me in against his chest. It felt comfortable, and right then I needed the comfort.

"Abby, you don't have anything to feel guilty about. You did what you had to do. You protected your family," Derek said.

"It doesn't feel that way. My dad just grabbed him and hauled him away. It's not right. His family doesn't know what happened to him or his brother."

I dropped my head into my hands, covered my eyes and wailed, "I killed his brother. I'm an awful person. That family probably doesn't know what happened to two of their babies! They are just missing and the not knowing has to be awful."

Derek gave me a firm shake. I lifted my head and looked into his dark eyes. He ran his thumb over my cheek and wiped away the wetness trailing down my face. "You aren't an awful person. You are one of the greatest gifts, I've ever found. You did nothing wrong."

"I killed..."

"Stop it," Derek interrupted. "You protected."

I shook my head and tried to make him understand. "It's eating me alive. I killed him. I have his blood on my hands."

I held up the palms of my hands for Derek to see. I know the blood had been washed away months ago, but I could still see the red of it. I could still feel the sticky of it. It felt heavy and thick.

"I took him away from a little brother who needs him. I took the very same little brother and helped kidnap him. He's locked away somewhere. I can't even go and see him. I want to try to explain. I want him to understand I did what I had to do, but..."

"Abby, stop. Stop." He took my hands into his and pushed them down against our legs and held them there. He pressed his forehead against mine and looked directly into my eyes, holding my gaze to him. I could feel him trying to make me listen, this time. Where I hadn't before.

"You were a part in the death of his brother, yes. Remember, you had no choice. That was clear self-defense. You didn't seek him out and just murder him. He attacked and would have killed you. This is the truth and you know it. Burn it into your mind and heart. You had to protect yourself and your family. Period."

"But..."

Derek shook his head and cut me off. "I'm not finished. The boy, he's half wolf. He's got a lot of the wolf in him and he will change. He will be a shifter. The Hunterz will destroy him for it. It won't matter if he's from them, too. All they will see is he is a shifter and they will kill him. We are going to help him. We are going to try to teach him the ways of the wolf."

"How? What will become of him?"

"That will be up to him. He's still angry. Combative. Silent. Once he gets through some of his emotions, we will be able to educate him. Teach him the ways of the wolf. Bring him into our world. He won't be alone forever. He just has to look, and he will see a whole clan is waiting to embrace him."

I wondered if he had one clan or two? Would the Grey clan embrace the boy as well? He was from the Hunterz. Would being a wolf taint him in their eyes?

"How long will he be secluded? When can I see him?"

I felt Derek hesitate to answer me. Why? I saw him struggle with an answer. He finally gave me the truth, even though he knew I wouldn't like it.

"I don't know. It will depend on him as much as the elders. He's angry right now. Unreasonable and destructive."

I would have been, too. Ripped from my world. Taken from my mom and my family. My brother killed right before my eyes. Yes, I'd be angry too.

"I don't blame him for his anger."

"No. I don't either."

We sat together and watched the rest of the sunrise together. When the sun was up in the sky and the light of the day lit the world around us, Derek stood and helped me to my feet. "Come back to bed. At least try to get a few hours in. It's a full moon tonight."

"Yeah," I said. I couldn't forget. It had been one month since that night. "I'm heading out to Lilly's."

Derek stopped walking. I halted as well and looked up at him. "Don't go this moon. Stay with me," he finally asked.

I wanted to, but there was also a part of me that didn't. "It's the first moon since Aunt Lilly balanced. I feel like I need to be with her."

After he didn't reply, I said, "Come with me, instead. You don't have to stay here. Make an excuse. Say it's to keep me safe. Say whatever you want, just come with me."

He laughed, more a deprecating laugh than one of enjoyment. "Look at us. Both wanting to go with the other and neither being able to. Too many obligations."

"But there's not. Come with me, Derek."

"I can't. I'm one of the adults and I have clan obligations on the full moon. You know this. You just don't like it," he said.

No, I didn't like it at all. They were stupid obligations in my opinion. As always, though, in the clan of males, my opinion and wants didn't count for shit. We reached the back door of my grandfather's home. Before Derek opened the door, I stopped him one last time. "Will it always be like this?"

"Like what?"

"Neither of us getting what we want? The clan always coming first? What I want or what you want not mattering at all to anyone but us? Putting the clan over our needs?"

I watched his face fall, "Don't do this, Abby."

"I'm not doing anything," I replied, but I was.

I wasn't born into the clan like he was. My motto wasn't clan first above all else. I didn't want to live the rest of my life having to be second.

He sighed then opened the door for us to go inside. "Let's go to sleep. Everything will look better once we've rested a bit."

I let him lead us up the stairs and I even allowed him to tuck me into my bed. I had a feeling nothing would look better, nothing would change. The question circling around in my head though was, what was I going to do about it?

Chapter Two

"No, thank you," I said from across the little kitchen table to Derek.

"Why is it every time, you get this way over your parents?" Derek said.

"Get what way?" I said as if I had no idea.

"Really?" Derek said and raised one of his perfect dark eyebrows. "Let's see. You refuse to visit with them unless you are forced, guilted, or have to."

"The door works both ways," I interjected.

"You don't even ask about your mom and how she is doing."

"She's about to have a baby, I know how she's doing," I said.

"You make everything so hard," he said. Derek sat quietly, giving me a full chance to answer.

"No, I don't. *They* make it hard."

"How?" he said and stared me down.

Like I didn't have a ton of reasons. "Hello, I was sixteen and pretty much booted out of my own house. I am an unwanted reminder to them, and they show it by never coming to see me. They didn't even come to my graduation. I have been left to flounder about in this whole wolfy world almost on my own, and they are trying to pair me up with their pick of wolf men."

"You like their pick of wolf men," Derek said with a big toothy smile.

"That's beside the point. What if I didn't? Let's face it, you were not my idea of perfection at the beginning. We have both come a long way and that's no thanks to them at all. So, yeah, I do have plenty of reasons."

"Okay, my turn," Derek said. "Things were weird at the start with your dad and mom and even me. I get it, but they didn't boot you out. You left." He held up his hand when I started to interrupt, and I fell silent, and let him continue. "You mom has been going through a hard time. Two pregnancies so close together, with a shifter, is hard, let alone at her age."

"Those were her choices."

"Maybe they were, but they took a toll on her and your father. Being so sick and so tired and everything else that comes with carrying a shifter baby, maybe you could cut her a little slack. Step into her shoes a bit and maybe find some compassion."

"Hey. I'm compassionate." I was getting annoyed.

"As for your graduation," he continued, "you and I both know your mom was sick, so sick she couldn't get out of bed to come. Your father was taking care of your little brother, and your mother as well, on his own. He couldn't come. Instead of you understanding and realizing it didn't have anything to do with you, you made it all about you."

"It was my graduation. It was about me!"

He sat there in his chair all high and mighty talking down to me and taking their side. "You always side with them." I stood up and leaned over the table, so my face was closer to his. "You always tell me to put myself in their place and see how they feel. Who does that for me? No one. Not one person. Not even you. Sometimes it is about me. My feelings count, damnit!"

I whirled away from the table and stalked up the back stairs to my room. I slammed my door closed, hard, behind me and turned the lock in place. Just once I'd like to be important. Just once. "No, it's never about me. My feelings are not worth an ounce of time to anyone." I looked around my room and realized I didn't want to be cooped up inside suffering my hurt feelings.

I changed into a pair of shorts and a loose tank top, and quickly tied my hair back into a pony tail. I grabbed a pair of flip flops, my keys, my wallet, and I left, not just my room, but the house as well. No one stopped me as I went out to my car. It could have been because no one saw me, or it could have been because they could see the steam rising from me, I was so angry.

After situating myself in the car and driving out onto the main road,

I could still feel the anger simmering in my gut. I hit my hand on the steering wheel. I didn't believe I was selfish. I gave up so much after finding myself thrust into the wolf world. How much more of myself was I supposed to give?

I stopped at a stop light right in the center of town and didn't know which way to turn. I had nowhere to go. I couldn't go home, as Derek would still be there. I couldn't go to my parents as I was still mad at them. A brief memory of William drifted through my head, but I quickly pushed the thought aside, too. He was out of the question.

My school friends from both clans were busy getting ready for college, and frankly me being a girl didn't seem like it should be an issue, but it was sometimes. Especially right now as I had a feeling my *season* was on its way. Yay me.

Being in heat meant I was better off staying as far away from the males, any males, wolf or otherwise, as much as possible. There were so many things that were awesome about being a wolf shifter. There were others though, that sucked. The whole going into season like a dog was one of the few I was not a fan of.

I looked around the small town. I could go to the library, but I wasn't in the mood to read. I looked right and saw the pizza place. As my brunch had been interrupted by Derek with his unwanted and unasked for opinion, I was hungry.

I pulled into the parking lot, and made to go inside, when I saw the red advertisement sign in the window. I continued in and sat in seat in a booth by the window. The place was almost empty, but considering it wasn't quite noon yet, I figured the place would be busy soon enough.

I looked out the window and thought about the budding idea in my head. I hadn't decided what to do with myself. I knew I wanted college, but where? I knew I'd have to figure out a way to get to college on my own, as if it wasn't an approved course of study at an approved school, I would have to pay for it on my own.

How did I know this? All the guys I'd graduated with were all going to the local community college. They were all taking one of four types of majors: finance, IT, software design, or business. There were no creative outlets available to our kind apparently. It didn't make any sense to me either. We were not poor. Our families all took care of each other. No one in the clan went without.

Maybe if I'd wanted to be a doctor, I would have gotten approved, but I didn't want to be a doctor. I wanted to go into animal studies. Bringing my choice of courses up hadn't gone great either. You would have thought I'd wanted to become a satanic priest the way everyone flinched away from my dream. Even my friends were wary of the idea. My last and only hope was going to be my great aunt Lilly. She, of all people, should support the idea.

Just in case though, I needed to come up with some other resources. I glanced around the pizza place once more, seeing it was still empty but for the staff, I decided it was as good a time as any, and stood up to speak with the manager about the job they were advertising. Any job would be a start, especially when I'd never worked before in my life.

I left the pizza place with not only a better frame of mind, but with a job in hand.

From there I went over to the community college. I figured if I were out to change my future, now was as good a time as any. I didn't have an appointment, and I didn't even have a plan, but I figured, why not?

I stepped inside an old brown brick building. It smelled a bit like dirt and mold. It felt cool within the walls. I didn't have any idea where to go. Thankfully, a dark-haired boy about my own age walked toward me in the dimly lit hallway.

"Excuse me," I said.

He stopped. He focused in on me. His face bloomed into an enormous toothy smile. The smile made me hesitate. It was creepy. "Um…is there an office here?"

I didn't have any experience at colleges. I didn't know if they had a main office or not.

"Sure, I'll take you over," he said and reached out to take my arm.

I stepped back just out of reach and turned in the direction he was pointing and said, "Great. Lead the way." I added in a smile to alleviate the possible insult of not wanting him to touch me.

His smile stayed in place. As it was giving me the willies, I wasn't certain that was a good thing. "My name's Brad," he said.

"Abby," I replied. I had a moment of worry, maybe I should have used a fake name. I let it go though, since there had to be plenty of Abbys in the world.

He chatted me up on the short walk to the administration building with the usual questions: "Are you from here? Are you thinking of going to school here? What will you study?"

I tried to answer simply, but politely, all the same.

Finally, he said, "Here you go."

We were standing before a door that said simply, *Admissions*. Awesome.

"Thanks," I said and turned to leave him where he stood.

I wasn't fast enough. He stopped me by taking my hand and saying, "I'll wait here for you."

Great.

I stepped through the door and to the first desk, where an older woman sat. Her brown hair was up in a sloppy bun which worked for her. She wasn't skinny, but not overly overweight either. She was dressed simply but professionally, and her genuine smiling face made it easier to approach her. "Hi," I said, "I'm interested in taking some classes in Animal Science. Is there someone I can speak to?"

"I'm sorry, but as we are in the summer session, we are short-staffed in that department. However, they will be back in August. I can schedule an appointment for you and I'm sure we can get you set up and going before fall session begins. You can also set up an appointment over in the Testing Center for your academic placement tests, cultural awareness inventory, gender sensitivity training, political proclivity assessment, career pathways recommendation assessment, and our Institutional Total Quality Survey. Oh, be sure to fill out the FFSA online so you can apply for financial aid."

Disappointment felt heavy on my heart for a moment, but I pushed it aside. I was a bit overwhelmed by all the steps it took to attend school, but whatever. It wasn't a wasted trip. It was a start. I quickly made an appointment with a counselor for August, said goodbye and left the office. I thought I might take a little tour of the campus, maybe get a soda at the Student Union if it was open. After that, I could go by the Testing Center to make other appointments. I made a quick note on my phone to check into that FHA or FFA or FFSA thing.

I stepped right into Brad. Ugh. I'd already forgotten him. "Oh, Brad. Sorry, I didn't see you there."

He laughed this throaty sound. It felt dark and slimy. It slithered down my spine and settled in my gut. I had a feeling he'd intentionally stepped into me, just for the chance to have my body against his, no matter that it was only for a moment. "No problem."

I tried to step around him, but he again took my hand. He really needed to stop doing that. "Can I have your number? I'd love to go out sometime."

Awkward…and no. "I'm sorry, Brad. You seem really nice, but I have a boyfriend."

His hand holding mine tightened its grip. Painfully. I tried to wiggle it out, but the struggle just made him hold tighter. "You're lying," he said, and tried to pull me in closer.

I moved as far back from him as I could, all the while I tried to get my hand free. "No. I'm not. I really do appreciate your help, though."

He stepped back in close to me.

I edged away again, and he came forward, until my back was against the wall across from the admissions door. Could the woman inside see us? I craned my neck around to try to see into the window of the door, but the angle was wrong. If I couldn't see in, she certainly couldn't see me.

I felt my wolf get testy. More of an annoyed feeling than angry. That all changed in a heartbeat the moment Brad pushed the length of his body up against mine and shoved his head and face a breath away. "Let go, and back off," I growled.

The sound of my voice should have been warning enough, but apparently Brad was not all that smart.

"No," he said and tried to press his lips against mine.

Oh, hell no. The thought was both a human and wolf response. Although I couldn't exactly shift into full wolf right there in the building hallway, I could pull the strength of the wolf forward. It wouldn't be the same as being a wolf, but it should be enough to teach him a lesson.

I reached down with my one free hand and grabbed the very tender spot on his body and…squeezed. "I don't think you heard me, Brad. Let.

Go."

The instant intake of a harsh breath was all the proof I needed. I had his full attention. His hand instantly released mine and he tried to step away. As I had a hold of a very dear part of him, he couldn't do so.

I leaned forward so I could whisper in his ear, more for dramatic affect than for fear of anyone hearing. "Women don't like to be manhandled, Brad." I punctuated my words with a bit of a squeeze.

He stopped breathing for a moment. I must admit I was enjoying myself. "You should know, I will be coming to this school. I really like the campus, and most of the people I've met. If I hear even an inkling of a rumor you are treating anyone, girl or boy, with less than the respect they deserve, I will hunt you down and finish this little thing we have going on right now."

I again gave him a squeeze.

He had blue eyes. I hadn't realized it until that moment. Maybe it was because they were currently as big as saucers, but regardless, I had his full attention. "Do you understand me, Brad?"

It felt good to know I was able to take care of myself on my own. I was in control. It was a heady feeling.

He nodded his head.

I could have made him say it. It would have been easy, but I figured I'd won. I didn't need to rub his face in it any more than I already had.

"Good," I said and released him.

He immediately stepped away from me. He didn't stop either. He turned and hurried away without another glance or another word. I watched him move past another building. I noticed the sign said *Testing Center*. Good. Well, Brad, oddly enough, even in his current condition, helped to show me where the building was located. I laughed. The sound echoed down the hall almost like it was chasing him away. Boys. Shifter or just human, they were all the same.

Smiling to myself, I headed toward the snack bar in search of a cold drink. After I finished my drink, I would stop at the Testing Center before heading home. It'd been a good day. I was really looking forward to attending college.

~ * ~

"What do you mean, you got a job?"

"Have you been sitting here all day, waiting for me to get back? Don't you have your own job to get to?" I said.

Derek paced away from me. He pushed angry fingers through his hair, making the thick mane stand up at attention. It made me smile to see the disorder on him. He was too perfect some days. It annoyed me. "That's not the point," he said.

"Look, I'm eighteen," I said.

Derek interrupted me and said, "Not yet, you aren't."

I took in a slow breath trying to hold onto my temper. "Fine. I'm almost eighteen. I have to start taking some control of my life. One of the things to get a handle on is my own finances. I can't live here forever."

Actually, I could. What I should have said was, I didn't want to live there forever, but even that wasn't quite right. I loved the family house, with the big rooms and the beautiful library. Even more so than I did when I first moved in, as I'd been able to brighten the place up a bit from the dark dreariness it had once had.

"Which means I have to get a job. I have to start making my own money. I've never held a job before, it's not like someone was going to offer me a six-figure job to start out."

"Your father would have given you a starting job," Derek said.

"Exactly. One more thing handed to me that I didn't earn. I'm not going to be beholden to anyone, especially my father. Ever. No one is going to take any of my hard work away from me and claim it for themselves."

"He wouldn't do that."

I shrugged, as truthfully, I didn't know if he would or not, but I wasn't taking a chance. "I don't want to go into the financial world, Derek," I said.

"You aren't still on the animal thing, are you?"

His tone, along with his words, set my teeth on edge. My temper, already simmering, bubbled even closer to the surface. A low rumbling growl slipped out.

Derek swung his gaze directly to my face and finally took note of me. Derek has a way of looking at people, but not actually seeing them. He was seeing me, finally. Good.

"Yes," I said through very clenched teeth. My hands were in little tight fists at my sides, as I tried to hold onto the last shred of my anger. "I am still thinking of the animal thing, also known as animal sciences, such as zoology, or animal biologist, maybe even a vet, big and small animals alike. Why is that such a problem? Why, Derek?"

"We are not like other humans, Abby."

As if I didn't already know it.

"We can't bring any type of suspicion on us. We don't want people in the medical fields, because of the possibility of our race being found out."

"We have a doctor in our clan. He's the one all the pregnant women have to see. So, don't tell me we don't allow it. Maybe it's because you don't allow the females."

"This isn't male or female," Derek said.

"Oh, sure it isn't," I said dripping with as much sarcasm as I could. "Everything in these clans is male and female oriented. Everything. Besides this isn't the medical field. This is animal science. Yes, it could be medical, but it's not on us, people. It's studies on all animals. I don't know what the big deal is. It's not like I am going to be experimented on while I study. Are you saying we have no one? Not one person has become a vet or something along those lines? Not one single person in the whole of the clans?"

"You are being difficult on purpose," Derek said.

Which meant to me, he had no idea how to answer the question. "Here's one for you then, as most of the girls aren't actual shifters and therefore are not of the higher race, why can't they be in the medical field then?"

Silence greeted my question. That was more proof to me, it was in fact a male female thing. "I guess I will be keeping my job then. I will need the money to put myself through school."

Derek stepped right into my personal space then. I didn't take it as an intimidation tactic. Not that he didn't sometimes try to, but right then, he wasn't. It was more of an I need to be closer to you kind of thing.

"Why is everything always a fight with you?" He asked the question to me, almost on a whisper of sound.

"I'm not trying to be difficult," I replied as I leaned into his body. It was a warm, almost summer day, but feeling the warmth of his body soak into mine calmed my temper more than any discussion ever would.

"Why is this so important? This animal science idea?" He wrapped his arms around my waist and settled his hands on my hips.

I decided to give it to him honestly. "I think we, as in the clans, should have some education on animal science as well as human science. We are both. Maybe if we understand both species, women will be able to carry babies easier. Maybe our children won't have such a hard time with normal sickness. Maybe there is a correlation we can find within the two species, both human and wolf, and that we are missing that will help our children when the change takes them. There are so many things we are missing because we are ignoring our animal side and trying to fix things as if we are just human."

Derek rested his chin on my head. I could feel the vibration of his voice as he said, "Does this have anything to do with your mom?"

I never said Derek was stupid. He could put things together faster than a lot of others I knew.

"Partly." That was as much of an answer as I was willing to give.

Saying out loud that seeing my mother so sick each time she was pregnant made me more afraid than I wanted to admit to myself, let alone to anyone else. It was more than only that selfish reason though. If all the non-shifter women went through this, we needed to find out why and how to help them. The one shifter doctor we had just took it as an absolute. When women were carrying, they were sick and sick and sick. They would either get over it, or they wouldn't. I wasn't going to allow the carelessness to continue. Not if they ever expected me to have children. "Do shifter women have as hard a time carrying babies as the non-shifters?" It suddenly dawned on me I had no idea.

"I don't know. You are the first shifter girl…in forever. You should ask one of the older generations."

I nodded, bumping his chin on my head a bit with the motion. "Lilly. She could tell me."

"There you go."

We stayed in each other's arms for a bit longer, just enjoying the feel of the other. There were many things about Derek that made me want to tear his face off, but there was something else in there which drew me in like a moth to a light.

"Are you getting close to your time?"

And then there was that mouth of his. I jerked back out of his embrace and snarled, "Seriously?"

"What?"

"You don't ask a girl that!"

"Why not?" he asked.

"Because. You just don't. It's rude."

"Well, considering the ramifications to others when you go into it, it's a good idea to let me know. I need to be prepared for the hordes of guys coming for you as well as to figure out how to keep myself in check. It's rude not to give me fair warning."

"Ugh." I spun around and stepped up onto the stairs to escape the embarrassing inquisition. Derek had other ideas. He wrapped a hand around my arm and turned me around to face him.

"Before you go," he said as he lowered his mouth to mine.

My anger melted out of me with the first touch of his lips against mine. That was why we worked even when I was mad at him. There was something going on with us and the something was stronger than anger. Whatever it was, it helped get us through the harder moments. Kissing was a definite bonus.

After we finally pulled back from each other enough to breathe, Derek said, "So, tell me about this job."

I smiled. There was another good thing about Derek, he could be cranky and bossy, but he would also stop and listen. "Okay, so it's at the pizza place in town and all I will be doing is cashing people out and taking their orders. I don't do the cooking or anything, but I'm fine with that. It's only part time and I told them it was most likely just for the summer."

"Doesn't sound too bad. When do you start?"

"Monday," I said.

I was actually excited about it. My first job, and, I'd gotten it on my own.

Derek leaned in and nuzzled my neck. He nipped me almost to the point of pain. I yelped and pushed him back. "Stop," I said all the while laughing.

"You smell really good right now. I love when you start to get close to your heat."

It was as his words sunk in that I deflated just a bit. I thought back to the moment in the pizza place when I asked for the manager. A man about forty came up and introduced himself as Kevin and he smiled. When I said I was there about the job, he didn't even ask me any questions, not even my name, before he said I had the job. I needed to come into the back and fill out paperwork.

Nothing happened really while I was completing the employment forms, other than his hovering about, but now that Derek mentioned my scent was changing, I knew the change had just as much effect on human males as it did shifter males. My hormones got me the job, not really me. Great.

"What's wrong," Derek asked.

I shook my head and said, "Nothing, I just realized I am going to have to tell my new boss I will have to take a few days off in a week or so to visit my aunt." Can't run around here with my *I'm fertile* smell infecting everyone. Just wonderful.

Chapter Three

"Hey, Gpa. Looking as dapper as ever," I said.

I found my grandfather in the library, which just happened to be one of my favorite rooms as well. He was sat on the chaise by the window, with a book in hand, which was also one of my favorite places to pass the time. He was dressed relatively casually for him, in a blue golf-type shirt and khakis. Usually, he was a full suit and tie type of guy. Normally, I would not have interrupted him while he read, as I hate that, but I hunted him down for a reason.

"What do you need, Abigail?"

"Do I have to have a reason to say hello?"

"No, but you have a tone. I know you well, my dear."

"Well, it just so happened I was looking for you," I said.

I gave him one of my most innocent smiles and plopped myself down next to him. Almost on top of him actually. I wanted him to make room for me, which he did by scooting over a bit.

"And…"

"Well, you see, I've been thinking about the boy. The one we took that day at Aunt Lilly's?"

"Yes, I know which one you mean. The shifter who is also one of the Hunterz. Yes. I know."

He spoke all the while keeping his eyes on the pages of the book he was pretending to read. I say pretending, as he hadn't turned the page since I walked in. He was pretending to not be interested, but he was. I knew him pretty well by then, too.

"I want to go see him. Will you tell me where he is being kept?" I asked it bluntly.

There was no reason to sugarcoat the request.

"No."

That was all he said. No explanation came with the one-word answer. "Why not?"

I didn't demand an answer. I just asked it.

I wasn't sure he would give me the why, but he surprised me when he said, "He needs time to adjust. He needs to understand his place in our world and accept it before we start bringing in other people."

"I understand why you would think that, but he's little. He's all alone and surrounded by strangers. He knows me. I want to help. Please."

One thing about my grandfather, he wasn't mean to be mean. He always had a reason for doing all he did. He may be wrong in his reason, but he always had one. It was a great attribute of most of the wolves. Took a bit of getting used to, but once you put aside the notion that they were intentionally offensive, it made dealing with them a lot easier. Well, most of the time. My father didn't fall into that grouping. It didn't matter that he was the same way; it felt personal when he did it.

He snapped his book closed and stood up. I watched him as he walked over to the big desk at the far end of the room. He pulled out a small tablet and wrote on it a moment. He carefully tore out the piece of paper, folded it once, then again, and walked back over to me, where I still sat. He held out the folded square, which I took. Once it was out of his hand and into mine, he turned and walked directly out of the library without a word.

I unfolded the note and felt a smile bloom across my face. My grandfather was wonderful. There in my hands, on the paper, were three short lines of an address. That was all. It was all I needed. My argument of why I wanted to go was listened to, contemplated in the span of a minute, and agreed with.

I ran out of the room, and made my way to the address, which was only about ten minutes away.

I pulled into the short driveway to a smaller home. It was a one-story ranch, with blue siding and a one-car garage. The house looked so normal. To be holding a small boy as a prisoner, that is. I walked up to the door and knocked. My hands were a little sweaty, I noticed. I rubbed them down the front of my jean-covered legs and waited. I could hear movement behind the door, but it still took several minutes for someone to open the door.

A very big male shifter opened the door. I admit to being momentarily afraid. He was a giant compared to me. He was also so muscular he could win one of those strong man competitions easily. His face was angular and evidently unhappy to see me there.

"Hi," I said.

He didn't return the greeting. I swallowed my nerves. I had been given permission to be there. I wasn't going to be frightened away. "I'm here to see Sam."

"Who says?" he said. His voice was so deep and so firm it actually made my legs shake a bit.

I cleared my throat of the sudden thickness coating it and replied, "I know you know who I am. My grandfather said I could come. Step aside and let me in."

I held his eyes with my own and refused to allow him to see how intimidating he really was. He probably already knew anyway.

He stared me down. I was beginning to think he wasn't going to let me in after all. It's not like I could have shoved my way inside with him blocking the door. He was just too big. After the longest staring contest I ever took part in, he finally moved from the door and let me in.

I stepped into one big room. It was both living room and dining room in one. The kitchen was just beyond, separated by a half wall. Off to the left was a hallway I assumed was where the bedrooms were. I didn't see any sign of a young boy. "Where is he?"

"Downstairs."

"Okay," I said and waited for him to show me the way. "Not much of a talker, are you?" I said it to partly annoy him and partly to break the heavy tension in the room. It didn't work as he didn't respond to me.

On the far side of the kitchen was a doorway. It looked perfectly standard but for the keypad on the wall next to it. I watched muscle man key in a number, making note of the code, which by the way was: one, two, three, two, one. "Wow, hard code you have there. How can you possibly remember it?"

A grunt was the reply given.

I heard a click of the lock and we went down into quite the set-up.

It was one giant room down there. A bathroom with shower stall was off to the side, but there wasn't even a door or walls to give it a bit of privacy. It was just put discreetly in the far corner. There were very few pieces of furniture. A double bed, a dresser, a small futon couch and a TV stand with TV. Lot of room wasted for the purpose it was being used for.

Sitting like an angry pit bull on the futon was Sam. His eyes shot daggers at both me and Mr. Muscles. His face was red with emotion. "What do you want?" It was snarled at me with such venom it took all my control to not step back from him.

"I thought you might like some company."

It was all I could come up to say. He was so angry. His arms were crossed tight across his chest and his shoulders were hunched against the world. I felt many emotions seeing him there. One was guilt for not coming sooner. One was sadness, because I felt partly responsible he was there. Another one was anger at the clan for the situation. Lastly, I felt sadness for him. Maybe he was there because of me, but he was also there because of himself. We had a lot to work on.

"I don't want you here. Get out."

I tried to come off as nonchalant when I shrugged one shoulder lazily at his response. Pretend as if I didn't care, even though his words did slice me a bit. "No. I came a long way to check on you. I think I'll stay a few minutes."

He actually turned completely around on the futon and faced away from me. Petulant. That was the word which came to mind. It made me smile even while I was uncomfortable. I turned to my escort and said, "Why don't you give us some space? Go get something to eat or lift some weights somewhere."

I heard a quiet snort from the child pretending to ignore me. It was a start. Not a great start, but it was a start.

"I am not sure about leaving you alone with him," he said.

"Well, I am. Beat it."

He looked from me to the child then back to me again. "I'll be right up those stairs. Give a shout if you need anything."

"Will do," I said as I watched him finally leave me and Sam alone. Which brought me to the next problem. Now what do I do?

Sam still didn't look at me. I was a bit at a loss as to what to do from there. "Not bad digs," I said, which sounds stupid the moment the words left my mouth. "It's better than what you are used to, I hope at least." As he'd come from a very unkept and broken-down trailer, the basement rooms were a huge step up. The drawback was, and even I was able to admit it, he could leave and do whatever he wanted at the old broken-down trailer in the woods.

Still nothing. I slowly stepped over to where he was sitting on the futon and sat down on the end. "Look, I know this isn't great. I know you don't want to be here. How can I help you?"

He turned blue eyes squinted almost closed in furious anger on me and said with more venom than a rattlesnake, "You can take your ass out of here and leave me alone."

I'm not sure what I was hoping to get from him, and maybe I should not have been surprised from the anger, but it hit me harder than I wanted it to.

He shut down and turned away from me. There wasn't much I could say to him right then. He was too upset and too closed off. I sat quietly next to him for a while. I don't know how long. It felt like forever and a day, but most likely it was only about half an hour. I tried to think of something to say that would help, but my brain was blank.

On a sigh, I stood up and made my way to the door. Before I left his little prison, I turned and looked at him, even though he refused to look at me, and said, "I'll see you tomorrow."

"Don't bother."

No, it wasn't what I wanted to hear, but he at least said something.

I headed back home and into the house from the back. I never really used the front door. The front entrance felt like the door for strangers or people who weren't entirely welcome. The back door felt like the family entrance. It opened up right at the kitchen, what felt like the heart of the giant house. Warm and welcoming is the best way to explain it.

The kitchen didn't disappoint either. It smelled of food. I sniffed the aromatic air and turned toward the little pot sitting on the counter. I lifted the water-coated lid. A plume of steam rose and hit my nose with the mouthwatering aroma of stew. It was the meat calling my name. Salty and spicy, it hit my system and made my stomach growl in want.

I put the lid back in place and stepped away from the pot. In general, I was a vegetarian. However, thanks to the wolf in me, staying away from meat was hard to stick with some days and the closer I came toward my season, the more I craved meat and lots of it. I still had a bit of willpower over it, though, which meant I had time before the craving hit in full force. I grabbed an apple from the counter, which was thankfully always full of some fruit or another and went in search of Derek. He should be home by now.

I found him up on the third floor, which was where his room was. I knocked on the frame of his open door. "Hey."

"Hey, yourself. How was the visit?" he asked.

I shrugged, not really surprised he seemed to know my every move. "Want to go for a run?" I asked instead of answering.

He inspected my face with his eyes and then said, "Yeah, I could use a run."

"Give me a few to get ready. I'll meet you out back, in say, five minutes?"

At his nod, I went back down to the second floor, where I dropped off my shoes and made a stop in the restroom before heading out back. Derek was waiting for me.

Without saying anything, we headed out toward where the forest met the open grassy area. As we got closer to the forest, the faster I walked. Derek picked up the pace as well. Soon we were running barefoot across the grass full out toward the trees. I was laughing freely. Derek looked at me with a full-on toothy smile. That moment was pure happiness.

As we neared the forest, I stripped off my shirt and shorts. Derek did the same. I hesitated to remove the last of my clothes, but it was necessary to shift. Derek didn't have any hesitation. He dropped his boxers and shifted in one smooth motion. I could do the same if I wanted, but not so much with an audience. As Derek was busy shifting, I also tossed my bra and panties and shifted quickly.

My body stretched and contorted to the shape of a wolf. A bit bigger than your standard, everyday wild wolf, and I was a beautiful one at that. Sleek shiny coat. My eyes retained the blue of my human self, so they were striking in my wolf form. I was pretty hot as a wolf. I just was.

Derek may be fine running about naked and free, but I was not. I wondered if I ever would be and would it actually be a good thing? Then all thoughts and worries were gone. We just ran. We raced through the trees. Jumped over obstacles made up of fallen branches and logs.

I felt elated and edgy at the same time. While in human form, I had more control of my emotions and feelings. In the form of my wolf it was more about instinct and needs. Like with meat, I could turn away from it without much issue as a human, but the moment the wolf came to the forefront, it was not as easy and in fact almost impossible. Food was not what my wolf was interested in though right then. The edginess in her was due to something way different.

The wolf and I were one being; we were one of the few shapeshifters who had been able to find a balance between the two entities. I was in fact the first, but my Great Aunt Lilly had been able to do it a few months back. This was proof it was possible to do, but so far, not many had. Two, in fact, had done it. Just two.

However, even with the balance, my wolf part and my human part, we each gave the other side more control depending on what shape we were using. As a wolf, I used the wolf's needs and instincts and allowed them to have more say as that was the wolf's area of expertise. As a human, the human needs and instincts took more power. The two sides intermingled well, but sometimes one side took control when it wasn't its turn, but for the most part, I handled both aspects well.

I had a vague feeling I was about to be a little out of my element. I was acutely aware Derek's wolf was right behind me. Almost on top of me. My body felt warm and my muscles were humming with tension. We were coming to a wide path and I slowed my pace to allow Derek to catch up and pace next me. I slowed us even more and moved in closer to him so I could brush my long body against his.

His dark face whipped around to stare at me. Wolves don't really smile. Even as a shifter, they don't smile. Our emotions and language are all in our eyes and our body movement. I turned my head just a bit to stare back at him, my head at a cocky angle and my eyes closing just enough to give off a sultry look. Or what I assumed was sultry. I hadn't exactly flirted before in the wolf form.

He came to a tripping halt. I came to a stop as well, but I circled him and again brushed my body against his as I went past. I flipped my tail over his nose and slowly let it slip over the broad flat of his muzzle. Derek was standing at attention. His body was stiff and still as stone. He tilted his head up and scented the air. It wasn't the quick sniff you would expect, but it was a long slow inhale. His eyelids lowered just before he shifted out of the wolf form.

Yeah, Derek had no qualms about being naked at all. I couldn't help myself; even in the form of my wolf, I could appreciate the fine specimen was Derek. From his feet, planted firmly on the dark pine-needled ground, up his muscled legs all the way up to his dark and currently wary eyes, with everything in between. Hoo, he was nice to look at. While in the wolf form, I wasn't as embarrassed to stare him down as I would have been as a human. There was something freeing as a wolf. I slid over to him and slowly brushed my soft fur from my neck to my rump against his legs. I allowed my tail to slide briefly around one knee before I pivoted and did it once again on the other side of him. As I was enjoying the soft pressure of his bare skin against my fur-covered body, Derek surprised me by squatting down and with a hand to my neck with gentle pressure, stopped my progress.

"Shift back," he said.

Usually he was all bossy and demanding, but the tone wasn't that. He was asking. I didn't want to, as although he was fine without a stitch of clothing on, I was not. As if sensing my hesitation, he added, "Please. We need to talk and it's easier with you as a human than a wolf."

I still hesitated. Shifting from human to wolf, I had this idea it was graceful and modest, as you were quickly covered in hair. When I'd seen others do it, it didn't look awkward and vulgar, it was exciting and beautiful all at the same time. You had the shifting from wolf to human and that didn't seem pretty at all. It had a clunky feel to it. I'd never seen myself do it and granted when others had, I admit to not really paying attention, but the feel of it was less than full of grace. I didn't want Derek to think I was afraid, though, as he had a way of appearing superior at times when it came to wolf things. I don't think he did it on purpose. It was just how he was.

No, I didn't like it, but I was beginning to understand him, though.

I mentally braced for the shift back. I then pulled the wolf in as I pushed the human out as fast as I possibly could, in order to get the awkwardness of it, over and done. I felt my feet flatten first, my back hunched, the fur was gone, and I was standing a bit too close to a very warm naked Derek.

Another great thing about the wolf genes, my hair was thick and very long. I fluffed it forward over my shoulders and used it like a screen for my chest. With my sight right on Derek, I said, "Eyes up here, big boy."

The grin he gave me was what I would term a wolfy grin. There were no other words for it.

I tried to stay still, but found myself fidgeting anyway. The warmth of his body was calling my name. I wanted to lean forward the scant inch it would take to press up against him. My entire being was suddenly focused just on that. How nice it would feel. How his skin would cause little shivers in mine. How the warmth would soak into my body. How...

"Hey...pay attention. I'm having a hard enough time keeping my hands to myself without you almost pouncing on me and staring at me with serious lust on your face that I want to pounce right back."

"What?" I said and forced myself to take a step back. "I didn't pounce on you," I said with as much distain as I could. "You wish."

"Seriously, Abby. You've got to try here."

He also took a step back. It was a very slow and stiff step, but he put more space between us. "My wolf is clamoring to be set free to take you. I'm holding on by a thread. You may have all this power and control over your wolf because of joining with her, but I don't. Frankly, you aren't showing a whole lot of control at the moment either."

I was speechless. I wasn't showing control? I thought back over the last few minutes and realized uncomfortably what he meant. I'd all but shoved my wolf butt in his face. That was why he'd shifted so fast. I had a semblance of control, but unbalanced shifters didn't. Their wolves were a force to be reckoned with. They were controlled by instinct. Their main focus was to eat, sleep, and procreate.

"I'm trying to give you time. I'm trying to not be pushy and demanding when it comes to sex and our relationship. The wolf doesn't understand relationships and not being ready. He smells your fertility and he wants."

I shook my head, more in shock at my stupidity than in denial. "I'm sorry." I turned away from him, in embarrassment. "This is all new to me. I'm just reacting sometimes, and it felt so good. I didn't think of how it would affect you and your wolf."

He released a breath. I heard him take in another and release it as well. "I know. I really do."

I turned back around to face him. "I'm not ready for wolf mating. Is that even a thing?" Then, "Wait, don't answer that. I don't think I want to know yet."

His short bark of laugher caught me off guard. "You are something else."

I smiled, sensing the tense moment was passing. I stepped close to him again. "Everything is so mixed up when I get this way. I know I'm balanced. Maybe that makes it easier, but it still feels hard. My body craves one thing and my mind shies away from it. Is it always this way?"

"I don't know how it is for girls. You should ask a girl. All I know is how I feel."

I stepped in closer, enjoying the quiet moment between us. My eyes were drawn to his mouth and I wanted his lips on mine. I wasn't sure how to go about asking for what I wanted. Did I just lean in and let him figure it out? I decided yes, that was the best course of action.

However, the moment my lips came in contact with his soft delicious ones, a sharp stabbing pain bloomed on my shoulder. I jerked back away and reached up to find the reason for the sudden pain and came in contact with a small cylinder stuck into the meat of my shoulder. I grabbed it and pulled it up between Derek and I and just stared at it. "What the hell is that?" I finally managed to say.

Derek took it out of my hand and his eyes were suddenly wide and very angry. "It's a dart."

Maybe to an outside person, the tone of his voice would have been fine. Conversational even. That was not what I read in his tone at all. The tone said rage was boiling up in him and he was pretending to be fine.

My body was feeling sluggish and the edges of my vision were blurring. "What do you mean a dart?"

My brain, along with my body, was slowing down. I couldn't comprehend what he meant. I reached out a hand to place on his shoulder to steady myself. I tried to shake my head to clear it, but the dark fuzzy edges were widening. "Derek," I said, not even trying to mask my growing apprehension.

He grabbed both my shoulders in each hand and held me steady. "Can you still shift?"

Could I? No. I was going down and going down fast. In fact, I didn't even have time to answer before the darkness took over completely and I was out for the count. The last sight I had was of the forest tilting and Derek shifting to wolf on a growl. The vicious growl echoed in my head even as I lost consciousness.

~ * ~

My next thought was, ow…my head hurts. It took another few moments to remember what happened. It took another few to realize I was in a soft comfy bed, with clean-smelling sheets tucked up around me. I was also naked. That last thought is what had my eyes finally opening.

I was then thoroughly confused. I was in my own bed, in my own room. Aside from a headache, a doozy of a headache at that, I was fine. I tried to sit up and the pounding in my head only intensified. "Nope, not ready to get up," I said to the empty room as I flopped back down.

I stayed there for a long moment. I came to the conclusion I either needed to die from the pain, or I needed to gather myself and get up to find some aspirin or something. It was a tough choice, but I finally opted to get up. I took it slow the second time, though. Easing myself into a sitting position, then slowly standing on wobbly legs.

I made my way over to my dresser and grabbed clothes. I was pulling down my tank top when the door opened. Usually I would have been a bit more vocal on the entrance to my room minus a knock, as I wasn't quite dressed, but I didn't have it in me to complain right then. "Derek, thank God. Can you get me something for my head? I think it's going to explode."

He turned and left without a word and returned a moment later with two tablets and a glass of water, which I quickly downed both before dropping myself back into bed. I closed my eyes to try to wait out the time it would take for the meds to kick in.

As I lay there, I asked, "What happened out there? How did we get home? Were you hurt?"

Derek sat down on the end of my bed and took my feet into his lap. He ran warm rough hands up and down my calves in a gentle caress. "I'm not sure what happened. It was strange."

"Strange, how?"

"You crashed, and I quickly shifted to wolf. I figured I would be better able to protect you in wolf form, but no one came. Nothing happened. I hauled you up on my back and brought you home. I didn't see anyone."

"What was the point of all that?" I asked.

Derek shrugged. "I don't know if you were hit with the tranq as a warning, or if I was meant to be tranquilized, which would have left you more vulnerable, but they missed, so they didn't do anything."

"You have no ideas?" If I didn't know the why, how would he?

"No. I called your father and grandfather over for a meeting. They will be here in about half an hour now. You should try to get moving."

Meetings. There were always meetings. "Why do I have to get up? I don't know anything," I said.

Why did everything need a meeting anyway? I understood it was serious. I mean, I'd been kidnapped once before, I got it, but why the big meet and greet over it?

"Can't you just deal with it?"

He lifted one eyebrow at me. The eyebrow meant many things. It was a 'seriously'? It was also a 'you know better than that'. I did. I really did, but I didn't like it.

"Maybe a shower will help clear my head a bit."

He helped me to my feet, then gave me a swat on my butt to move me along. "Get to it then. I'll meet you downstairs. Don't be long as you know how everyone loves waiting."

I glared at him as my response. He should have known better than to even try to order me about. I had a stubborn streak a mile wide.

A good forty-five minutes later, I padded down the stairs to the family room. My hair was still wet. I hadn't taken time to brush it into a semblance of order other than to tie it out of my face. Even so, I was clean and starting to feel more alive and in better spirits. I took a good look at the three men waiting for me.

I sat down in the chunky chair I loved. It was a lovely yellow color and full of fluffy comfy pillows. My grandfather let me pick it out when he finally allowed me to brighten up the room a bit. It had been grey and black. Not very inviting. It had taken me months of begging, but the effort was worth it. I'd had it repainted in a soft neutral yellow. The dark black furniture I'd put in storage and had it replaced with maplewood tables, and a more welcoming couch and love seat set of forest green. Its dark contrasting color complemented the walls and the tables. The chair, however, was mine.

The dour expressions on the faces of the men, though, was ruining the effect of the calming room. "Sorry to keep you waiting."

Derek shook his head and said, "No, you aren't."

He said it with a harsh tone, but his eyes twinkled at me. He knew exactly who he was dealing with. He was learning.

I shrugged one shoulder and moved my gaze over to my grandfather. "Don't look so dour. Everything worked out. We're fine."

Apparently, that was way not the right thing to say. My father stood and stalked over to me. He was a hard one to figure out. I would start to feel like we were making headway on a decent relationship, but it would always go to shit. We were currently in that type of moment. "Explain to me how everything is fine?"

It sounds like an easy question, but when it's shouted in your face, not so much. I pretended to not be affected by the screaming, breathing man an inch away, but inside I was a little shaky. My father was an intimidating man.

"Adam," I said. I liked to call him by his name just to annoy him. I don't know why. It just made me happy.

He snarled, the reaction I was hoping for.

"Everything is fine, because Derek is not hurt. I am not hurt. That should be the most important thing here." I was pretending to be reasonable.

The rumbled growls emanating from my father were my only warning that maybe he was not in the mood for my attitude. He snatched me up out of my chair so fast by my shoulders, I was left a little dumbfounded. I was dangling off the floor a foot or so and my father's angry face was a scant inch from mine. I could feel his misty breath on my cheeks.

Derek jumped to his feet and placed a hand on my father's shoulder. "Maybe we should take a breath."

I stared wide eyed at my father, not saying a word. He was more upset about the situation than I gave him credit for. That was my mistake. Sadly, it was a mistake I had made in the past and would most likely make it again. After a deep intake of air, my father lowered my feet to the ground and took a step away. "Why do you do that?"

The question took me by surprise. As such I answered truthfully. "I don't know. I wanted to see what you would do."

"Was that what you expected?"

He was looking right at me. It was a heavy weight, his stare, but it seemed genuine and for once he was actually seeing me. It softened me on the inside where I tried to stay hard in front of him. There was something about appearing weak in his eyes that I was not willing to do.

"No. I don't know what I expected. I'm sorry."

He nodded his head once, turned and went back to his seat. Derek followed his lead and retook his seat as well. That brought my attention to my grandfather. He hadn't moved from his spot on the loveseat. He watched the entire moment without motion or word. He looked from my father to me and said, "Are we finished with the dramatics? Can we get on with the issue at hand?"

My grandfather was something else. He could make you feel small in no time flat. "Yes," I said simply.

He stood. My grandfather, he was old world. It was a Sunday afternoon and he was dressed in a full suit and tie, for Pete's sake. He stood, and we all took notice. We all gave him our full attention. "So, it would appear the Hunterz are back to doing their dirty work. The question that remains is why and why now after they have been relatively silent for a few months."

"The answer seems simple," I said. "We have Sam. They must know we have him. They must know his brother is dead, and they believe we are to blame." Actually, I was to blame, but I wasn't quite ready to say it out loud.

"I agree with Abby," Derek said.

I smiled. Having someone on your side felt nice. Usually I was alone on my side, or so it always felt.

"So, the question then remains, what are we going to do about it?"

"Nothing," my father said.

My mouth hit the floor and I swear my eyes goggled out of my head. My father, the tough guy, protector of all, didn't want to do anything? Didn't want to go all he-man on me and order me to a convent? What was going on?

"Say again?" I said, my tone dripping in disbelief.

"They want the boy. We aren't going to give them the boy. We are going to pretend their little stunt was worthless to us and we didn't care at all. If they think it bothered us, they win. If they think it was a wasted effort, we win. I am not giving them any leverage against us. We will keep the boy. We will teach him our ways and he will become one of us. They can't do anything about that."

I hated to be the voice of opposition, but someone had to say it. "What if he doesn't become one of us? What if he learns all he can and goes home?"

"He can never go home."

That was from my grandfather. It was said with such finality I realized if Sam tried to go, he probably wouldn't survive the leaving.

I didn't have anything else to say. I decided right then and there, I was going to make sure Sam stayed. I was going to do all I could to get through to him. The word death was not said out loud, but I was not going to let a little boy, demon that he was sometimes, be destroyed. It was not his fault he was a shifter born to the Hunterz. That was the fault of the clans and the Hunterz. It was not his. I was going to make sure he didn't pay for their mistakes.

Chapter Four

Monday arrived and with it, my first day of my job at the pizza place. There had been a tense moment that morning when I had to leave. Both Derek and my Grandfather thought it would not be a good idea for me to be out and about on my own, thanks to the whole dart event. I reminded them I didn't do great with bodyguards. I left them both behind seething. It was not a great start to the day.

The first order of business was my uniform. Mustard yellow was not really my color. Oh, I loved yellow and usually liked the brown tint, but the mustard color of the crew neck shirt was a bit too brown against the yellow to make it a pretty.

Following that there was the fight with my hair. I have a lot of hair. A. Lot. It's very long and tends to be on the wild side. I had a feeling my hair issues were due to my wolf DNA. It grew too fast. It was so thick and heavy and wavy, it was a bit much. I admit it.

I was told by the assistant manager, Tammy, to tie my hair back, which I did. I quickly pulled it back into a pony tail and thought that was that. Again, Tammy demanded I tie it back more.

I smiled even though I was a bit annoyed. Not so much by the request, but by the tone. "What does more mean? I can braid it?" I asked in as benign a tone as I could. This was my boss for the day, so I didn't want to start out on the wrong foot.

"Bun it," she said and walked away.

I took in a deep breath. I wasn't sure how exactly to bun my hair right then. I had one pony tail holder. I'd have to make do. I took out the hair tie, twisted my hair and then it around the top of my head to form a bun, messy, but a bun all the same, then I wrapped the hair tie around it as best I could to secure it. I wiggled my head back and forth a time or two. It felt pretty secure. How it looked, I couldn't tell you, but it felt okay.

I was going to have a headache from hell later with all the weight on my head. Thankfully, my first shift was more of a watch and learn thing. It only lasted four hours. I could survive four hours. I wasn't sure I was going to be able to survive Tammy though.

My first impression of her had been she was a short little dumpling-shaped woman, with an unhappy chip on her shoulder a mile wide. She was going to make it a long day. Considering her terse voice and angry eyes, I had no doubt about it.

What was left of the morning and the early afternoon, passed quickly, if not easily. I'd washed dishes. I'd wiped down tables and booths. I took out the trash. I cleaned bathrooms. I swept floors. The job I'd been told I would have I received very little training on. Thankfully, I was a fast study and learned the cash register quickly. I knew Tammy would have taken great pleasure in correcting me. I know this as she hovered over me all day, making sure to critique every single thing I did.

She must have thought I never washed dishes or took out the trash before. I wanted to turn on her and give her a piece of my mind, at one point when she said, just under her breath, "Why do they stick me with these spoiled rich kids?"

I grew up average. Single mom, chores, budgets, the works. Even now, I wasn't rich. My family was, but I wasn't. Hello, that was why I had the job.

Thankfully, my shift ended at two and I was clocked out, my hair was down, and I was in my car not three minutes later. It had been a long day. At least as part of my pay, I received discounts on pizza. I had a large pepperoni pizza sitting on my passenger seat smelling up my car nicely as I pulled out of the lot.

Ten minutes later, I pulled into the driveway of the little ranch house. With the hot pizza in hand, I knocked on the door. Mr. Muscles was there to open it and scowl at me as he had the day before. I was about done with people for the day and his attitude was almost the last straw. "Are you going to let me in, or just stare at me?"

His mouth tightened in obvious annoyance, but he didn't say

anything. He did thankfully, step aside and let me in. I didn't waste any more time on him. Instead, I headed directly to the basement door. I'm sure a lot of people would say it was not a basement, it was downstairs. You can dress it up all you like, but to Sam, it was a basement prison I'm sure.

I entered the code, opened the door and went down. I heard the jailer up the steps close the door behind me. The 'snick' sound of the lock falling into place hit home the idea that gilded cage or not, it was still a cage.

I put on a fake smile that I hoped looked real, and said to the sulking boy in front of the TV playing a game on some type of gaming system, "Hey, I brought pizza. It's even fresh."

He didn't even look at me, but was happy to say, "Why do you smell like that?" There was such disgust in his voice it might have hurt my feelings, but as I had worked all morning and sweated my way through some type of initiation I didn't understand, I probably did stink.

"Sorry, I just came from work."

"Hmm," was all he said. It was more of a huff of breath than a sound, but it was at least a response. I set the box down on the little table next to the futon, within his reach, and flipped open the lid. The aroma of hot cheese, garlic, and pepperoni was heavenly to me. "I don't know about you, but I'm starving. So, if you want any of this, you better get it."

I munched on a slice, while I watched him. He didn't say anything at all. He was intent on the game. It was a shoot up the city type of activity. I wasn't sure I understood it. Why was the city his character was in destroyed, and why were there…zombies? After a few minutes, and when there was a pause in the game, Sam reached into the box and pulled out a piece for himself.

He crammed almost the whole thing in at once, left the tail of it hanging out, and went back to his game. After a few chews, he pushed in the rest. Ew. Boys are grosser than I thought. At least he chewed with his mouth closed, mostly.

"What is this game?" I asked.

Without taking his eyes from the game, he pointed at a box on top of the TV. I couldn't see it from where I was, and I didn't care enough to get up and look, so I let it drop.

I tried another tactic. "What's the object? Just kill all the zombies?"

"Duh," he said.

I was tired. My head was pounding. Everyone was crap to be around that day. I gave up on conversation for the moment and went back to eating. He took a piece every now and then. I ate a few myself. Before I realized it, the pizza was gone and there was nothing left for me to do with myself.

"Well, I guess I better get going."

"See you," he said.

Why did those two words, sound like such an attack?

"Yeah." I tossed the box in the bin by the bathroom and walked upstairs feeling more and more dejected the longer the day went on. I was getting nowhere with him. He barely looked at me, let alone talked to me. Well, other than to insult me.

I sniffed my shoulder as I left the basement and didn't smell anything. A bit of garlic maybe, but nothing horrible. "Do I smell bad?" I asked Mr. Muscles.

I apparently took him by surprise as in an unguarded moment, he smiled, just briefly, before the flat empty look was back in place. The smile made him seem more human, even if only for a moment.

"You smell like girl," he said.

"Is that bad though?" I persisted.

He shrugged. "Maybe to the young ones. The shifted will not find it bad. In fact, most likely just the opposite."

I was a bit thick sometimes, but suddenly like a dawning light snapped on in my face, I got it. Sam was smelling me as I was going into my season. "Oh my God!" I didn't think of him as a male, I just thought of him as a little boy. "That is so awkward. Why does this happen? It's so gross and so not fair." I had to stop myself as my voice rose by the moment and on each word.

All I got was an empty expression on his face in return of my rant. He was no help. "Great. Just great," I said, as I stomped over to the door and yanked it open to leave. Before I closed the door, I bark at him, "Do you have a name?"

"Tanner."

That was it. No, nice to meet you, even if it was a lie. Just the name, snapped out as if I'd ordered the word. As I was already mad, it just annoyed me that much more. I thought it better to just leave. I turned and closed the door without response and went home.

Monday sucked.

It didn't get much better. Thankfully, no one was about when I arrived at the house. I was able to go up and have a shower. I felt better after that. As I had the house basically to myself, I decided to go relax in the library. I pulled the book I started off the shelf, curled up on the chaise by the window, and finally, found a moment of peace in an otherwise long crappy day.

My quiet reading lasted all of an hour and a half. Derek came home first, my grandfather directly after. It was almost like they planned it that way as they converged on me not five minutes upon their arrival home.

"Derek stepped through the doorway first, and said, "I heard back from some of the other families. No one else has had any problems. No one has seen anything either."

"Hello to you too," I said, when he stopped talking.

He gave me a quick half smile, leaned over me, gave me a quick peck on my lips which was almost worse than no kiss at all and said, "Sorry, hello."

My grandfather came in the library and continued where Derek left off. "I contacted the Grey clan head today and they haven't had any issues over there either."

"You? You called the Greys?"

Derek sat down at my feet, took the book from my hand and closed it. I really hated it when he did that.

"Hey," I said and snatched the book back. Flipped through the pages until I found where I'd left off, then turned down the corner and stuffed the book under my leg.

"That bends the pages, Abigail. Please use a marker," my grandfather said. "Yes, in answer to your question, I did call. Talks are not as acrimonious as they have been in the past."

My quiet moment was over. I closed my eyes and tried to find the calm I'd just had a firm hold of.

"Yesterday was their first strike then," Derek asked.

"It appears so," my grandfather replied.

"Or, it was just a continuation from last winter. They struck, we took the boy, they retaliated."

"They don't know for certain we have the boy," Derek said.

"Oh, they know," I replied.

My grandfather took that moment to ask, "How did your visit with him go?"

"Yesterday or today?" I asked.

"Either."

"I guess it doesn't matter which day, they both sucked."

"Language, Abigail," he scolded.

"I'm sorry, but there isn't another word I could have used. He is unhappy. Doesn't talk to me. At all. I'm not doing any good, but I'm not giving up." Then, "Could you have found a more taciturn guard? Does the guy have any feelings at all?"

"Tanner is ex-military. He has a background we can use in this type of situation," he said.

"Tanner?" Derek asked.

"The guard at the house for Sam," I answered, then turned back to my grandfather. "Well, he and Sam are perfect for one another. I've spent at least five to six hours over there and had them speak maybe ten words to me together. It's lonely over there and I'm not even a prisoner. I can leave whenever I want."

"What's your point?" Derek said.

"My point is maybe Sam could use a bit of warmth in the house."

"Do you really think he had warmth or affection before?" Derek asked.

His words made me stop a moment. What did I really know about him? He came from a poor home, with a single mother, and one brother that I was aware of and which I just happened to have also killed. He spent a lot of time out wandering the woods, which is how I found him or him me in the first place. I didn't know anything more about his home life. "Maybe not, but that doesn't mean he couldn't use it now."

"What do you suggest?" my grandfather asked.

"Do you know any clan women who could go cook a decent meal and just be around a little bit? Soften the isolation a bit?"

"I will see what I can do."

As usual, there wasn't any need of argument with my grandfather. He listened and decided. That was it. "Thank you," I said. I stood up and gave him a hug.

He gave me a very brief squeeze in return then stepped away. He was not a touchy-feely kind of guy. I knew that, but I kept trying. Just like with redecorating the house, I was working on revamping him too. It was only a matter of time before I won that round too.

Chapter Five

Sadly, Tuesday was not any better at work than Monday had been. Tammy hated me. That was the reality of my job. I poured my tired body into my car after another long shift of being worked over by the assistant manager, which meant cleaning, mopping, cleaning, dishes, cleaning, and anything else she could think of to make me do. I fastened my seat belt, started the car, and left the lot before anyone could come and try to drag me back in.

I sighed long and loud in the silence of the car. I couldn't even complain to anyone about the job as no one wanted me to have it. Not Derek, who even though he wished me luck, didn't like me working at a non-clan establishment. He didn't understand I wanted to feel like I was making my way in the world on my own steam. If I went to a clan business, they would feel like they had to hire me because of who my grandfather was.

Tammy sure as heck didn't want me working there. That one I wasn't certain the why of. I did all she asked me to do, without complaint. She just hadn't liked me on sight. I would suck it up. I could get through a summer break. I could do this.

I simmered over my day all the way to my destination, which was not to visit with Sam that day. I decided to stop over and see my mother. It had been several weeks since I'd seen her or heard from her, so it was as good a time as any.

I pulled in the drive and saw my father's car was not in the drive, but my mother's car was. For once I really didn't know if that was a good thing or a bad thing. My relationship with my father was complicated but it was certainly better than it had been in the beginning. Two years ago, I would have been relieved to have my father gone.

I stood in front of the front door and found even though my relationship with my father was better, I still didn't know how to enter the house. Was I supposed to knock or not? I finally decided to try the handle. If it was unlocked, I'd just go in. If it was locked, I'd have to knock. I turned the knob and the door opened. "That settles it then," I said under my breath as I entered the house.

It was full-on summer and the sun was shining bright and warm, but the house was dark and cool, and...I sniffed the air. It was really smelly in there. What the hell was that? Garbage?

I stepped inside and instantly fell over something hard and small. I landed flat out on the floor with a loud thump, thankfully without too much damage. "Ow," I said and grabbed my poor toes which had plowed into whatever was on the floor in the doorway. I picked up the object and saw it was a metal firetruck, complete with side ladders and hoses. Nice.

I set it off to the side of the walkway and pushed back to my feet. I fumbled around for the light switch and flicked on the overhead light. "Holy crap on a stick," I said when I took a good look at the front room. It was littered with toys, chip wrappers, clutter, and debris. It was no wonder the house had an off stink to it. It was gross.

I stepped lightly out of the front room and into the kitchen, where I found more of the same, just add in dishes and old food. I slid my feet over the linoleum floor and found there was a slippery grit to it as well. "What is going on?"

Over in the corner was a trash bag, which needed to go out. Badly. There was an overflowing trash can next to it. The stove top was covered in used pots and pans. The sink was full of dishes and cups and glasses.

I covered my nose with my hand and realized this was where the smell was coming from. I looked through the doorway into the bathroom that was off to the side and saw the little room wasn't much better.

"Mom?" I yelled out into the quiet house.

Her car was there, but there was obviously no sign of her. I carefully stepped my way to the staircase and went to see if she was up there.

I glanced in my old room, which had been converted into Toby's room. It thankfully was not a complete pigsty, which was something at least.

I found my mother in her room. She was laying like death in her bed. Her skin was grey, and her hair was dirty and matted to her head. "Mom," I whispered.

She opened very bloodshot eyes to stare at me. "Are you really here, or am I still asleep?"

I carefully sat down next to her on the bed. I pushed a hank of hair out of her face and said, "I'm really here."

"I'm just so sick," she said. "The last time, it wasn't this bad. The sickness lasted a few months, but then I was fine. It's not going away with this baby." As if to punctuate her words, she jerked up and over the other side of the bed, where she proceeded to retch and retch whatever contents was in her stomach into a perfectly placed little trash can.

To say I was in shock would be an understatement. My mom was a mess. The house was a mess. It was really bad there. "You need a doctor," I said.

"He comes every day. There is nothing more he can do."

Nothing more he can do? Really? I was worried. I admit it. I'd seen her when she was so sick with Toby, but it didn't last. My mom was seven or eight months along now. Being that sick should have passed by then. "Where is Toby?" I asked after she had flopped back down on the bed and settled in.

"We started taking him to a childcare place for the day. I just couldn't…Adam didn't want to wear me out any more than I already am. It's better this way," she drifted off.

I didn't want to awaken her. She looked like she really needed the rest.

I made my way slowly back downstairs and looked around. There wasn't much I could do to help her, but I could help in at least a small way. I took the hair-tie off from around my wrist, tied my hair up in a messy bun and got to work. I washed dishes, I swept and mopped floors, I took out the trash, and cleaned all I could downstairs. The grit on the floor? That was cookie.

It took me two hours to get the place in a semblance of order. Once I finished, I left without saying a word to anyone about it. Let my dad think my mom did it, or my mom think my dad had. It would help. Even if it just helped with the stench of the place, it would help.

I had planned on only making a quick stop at my parent's house before going over to the ranch to sit and sulk with Sam while he ignored me, but after my day from hell at work, along with my cleaning frenzy at my mom's, I was exhausted. I went home instead.

I had literally just sunk down in a deep hot bath full of bubbles when the door to my bathroom swung open and Derek stalked in. "Hey," I shrieked as I hurriedly placed bubbles in strategic places. "You can knock!"

"I've seen it before," he said as if that made it okay.

"I let you see it before. I'm not consenting to it now. Get out."

He didn't leave. Instead he sat down on the closed lid of the toilet and said, "God, this has been a day. I just needed to see your face for a moment."

Well...all right then. I slide a bit further under the water and said, "You and me both. What happened with your day?"

"Your mom needs to have her baby soon. Your dad has been hell on wheels to be around lately."

That pretty much summed it up. Working for my dad was great for Derek as he loved my dad and would do anything for him. Idolized is a better word for how he felt about my father. If Derek said my dad was hard to be around, he had to be impossible.

"I can imagine," I said. After seeing the state of the house and my mom, it had to be bad. "I never asked, when is her due date?"

"Mid-August." He dropped his face into his hands and continued, "I'm not sure we are going to survive another two months."

"That bad?" I asked.

"That bad," he answered. Then, "How did your day go?"

I hesitated. I wanted to whine about how mean Tammy was to me, but I also didn't want to add to his long day. "It was okay, I guess. Long, tedious, and hard work, but it will get easier once I'm out of this training stuff this week."

At least I hoped it did. Considering how cranky Tammy was, it was amazing they had any other staff who would work with her.

"I'm glad you are sticking with it," he said.

"Yeah, sure." I knew how he felt about me working there.

"No, really. It's not what I wanted, and you know it. I'm still proud of you," Derek said.

I buried my smiling face in a mountain of white bubbles.

"I could use a wash too," he said suddenly getting to his feet. "Is there room in there for two?"

My eyes shot wide when I realized what he'd said. He was kidding…he had to be kidding, right? I sat up and sloshed water all over the place. He wasn't kidding. He was stripping off his shirt and kicking off his shoes.

"There isn't room in here. Derek!" His dress slacks dropped to the floor and his socks followed in little scrunched up balls to land in the pile he was making faster than I could even try to get control of the situation.

He left on his boxers. Not that it helped any. I didn't have any clothes on, so the fact he'd left a scrap of cloth on didn't amount to much. "There's room. Move over."

He stepped into the tub with one foot, then the other and I was at a complete loss as to what to do. "You can't…Derek!" He wasn't listening to me at all. He dropped his big long body into the water and made room. The fact that making room meant my legs were trapped under his and he was pretty much sitting on my feet, didn't seem to matter to him. Where I had been relaxed and easy, now I was as taut and anxious as possible.

"This is nice," he said and let his eyes fall closed. "Why are you staring at me?"

"You're in my bath."

"I'm not naked," he said with his eyes still closed.

He still looked relaxed and content. I, on the other hand, was as tense as you'd imagine. "I am," I said.

The wolfish smile that spread over his face, told me he was very aware of my situation. He confirmed it when he said, "I know."

I stared at him with my mouth open for another moment, before I decided if he wasn't going to make a big deal about it, then for once, neither was I. I settled myself deeper into the water. As I pulled more of the slowly dissipating bubbles up over me, I said, "Fine." I closed my eyes and tried to relax. It was the best I could do with the situation.

We sat quietly for a while. The water started to cool and what was left of my bubbles was more a foam than anything else. I eyed Derek to make sure he was still pretending to rest, before I stretched my arm out for my big fluffy towel, stood, and quickly wrapped it around me in almost one motion. If he got a good look at anything, it was quick and most likely wrinkled from the water. The idea of it all brought a smile to my face. I'd needed a relaxing moment. Although it hadn't felt like I got one, I had to admit I was in a better frame of mind than I had been, and I was happier. Maybe Derek knew more than I gave him credit for.

I went to my room to get dressed. I heard Derek leave the bath almost as soon as I was out of the room. I smiled my way through the rest of the day. Although the day had not been the greatest, it had turned into one that wasn't horrible. I'd take it.

The rest of the week took on a strange pattern I never would have expected. I'd go into work to open and train until two or three. From there I would stop at my mom's house, where I'd do a quick pick up. Thankfully, it was nowhere near as bad as it had been the first day. Wednesday and Thursday, I pretty much did a quick check on my mother who slept both days while I was there. I would do a hurried pick up and tidy before heading out again.

On Friday, my mom was up and about when I arrived there. She seemed confused and upset, but seeing her awake and moving around made me feel less worried than I had been. Honestly, I hadn't even realized I'd been stressed over her until I saw her, and I actually felt a weight lifted from my shoulders.

I was surprisingly quite happy to see her. at least I was, until she opened her mouth and said the moment I came into her view, "What are you doing here?"

I hesitated in the doorway and went from happy to see her to annoyed. Annoyed not just at her for her constant attitude toward me, but at myself too for expecting anything different. "You know, I think we get along better when we don't see one another and especially when we don't talk." I set my keys and wallet on the kitchen table and sat down opposite her. "I came to check on you. As I have every day this week."

"That was real?" she said. "I thought I was dreaming you."

"Nope, it was real." I didn't know what else to say so I sat and waited for her to move the conversation along.

She looked me over once, then directly in my eyes, before she asked, "Have you been picking up the place?"

I shrugged as if it was no big deal and said, "Yep."

She shook her head and said, "But why?" The movement of her head brought my attention to her hair which, like mine, was a bit on the curly side and usually very nicely tended. It was not so that day. It was shiny with oil, and a tangled matted mess.

I stood up and began to rinse off the dishes in the sink and place them in the dishwasher. "Someone needed to."

Although it had not been my intention, she took offense at my words and stood up on shaky legs to defend herself. "I can't help it. I can't do it all on my own right now. I'm sick and I'm just so tired. You don't know what it's like."

I didn't even really react to her little tirade. I continued with the dishes and spoke to her with my back facing her. "Sounds like you are the one with the issue. I didn't say a word about it. I stopped over to check in on you, thanks to less than gentle prodding of Derek and my grandfather, to find the house in a complete tip. I figured you could use the help, so I did. It's not that big of a deal."

When she didn't respond back, I craned my neck around to look at her, only to find her staring silently at me. It was disconcerting. "What?" I said.

"I remember so many things about you growing up. I remember how I felt and all the things we did, and how it was me and Abby against the world. I remember all of it, and when I remember, I miss you so badly when you are gone. Then you show up and although I remember how I felt, I don't feel it now. I know who you are. I know I how I should feel, but I just don't. I feel nothing."

A sharp knife of pain hit my chest and I flinched away from the pain of her words. They were spoken so nonchalant, but they had the sharpness of a dagger. I pulled a clean kitchen towel from the drawer and wiped off my hands. I was giving myself time to school my features and my turbulent temper.

"Well, thanks for sharing," I finally said. I headed out of the kitchen, picking up my keys on my way past the table, and out the door I went. My mother didn't try to stop me. She didn't say another word.

I calmly sat in my car and made the trip to the next stop on my list of things to do. When I arrived at the little ranch, I didn't even knock, I walked right in without a word to Tanner, who, although he seemed a little surprised by my entry, didn't stop me. Maybe he saw my face, maybe he felt my turbulent emotions, I couldn't tell you why. All I knew was, I was grateful. I didn't have a lot of energy left to deal with him.

I pushed in the code to the basement, and went directly down the stairs to the futon, where I dropped on the cushions with a huff. Sam, as if expecting me, sat right in front of the TV, a little too close if you want to know the truth, playing a video game. It wasn't the usual shoot everyone and everything thing. It was a car racing game. He pretended to not even notice me.

I honestly didn't care right then. My heart and soul were in turmoil. All the things my mother said were said with such honesty and truth and maybe a bit of sad confusion was added in, but the fact it was the truth, and it was so horribly mean, broke a little bit more of my heart. I could give her credit for the genuine confusion in her voice. I couldn't forgive her for the fact she said it. To my face. I was her daughter. We did have all those memories. We did have that past. We did have all those emotions, memories and feelings. The fact she could remember how it was meant she should do something about the disconnect now. That I should matter to her enough for her try, but I didn't matter, and she didn't try. So, there it was. I was just someone she used to love. Someone she used to know. Someone she used to...

"No pizza?"

I jerked out of my melancholy thoughts and focused in on Sam. "What?" I said.

"You didn't bring pizza," he said. He didn't bother pausing the game or looking at me. He just talked out into the space of the room.

"No. No pizza today," I said.

I took a good hard look at myself at that moment. What was I doing? Cleaning a house for people who didn't give a crap. Bringing pizza to a kid who didn't want me around. Working at a pizza place with a woman who was trying to make my life miserable. What was I doing?

"You should bring pizza if you insist on coming."

I stood up. "I don't know why I even bother," I said, more to myself than to anything. "I am not helping anyone. I thought I was. I was helping out at the house, thinking I was lightening the load and doing a good thing, but I'm not. I come here, thinking you could use a friend. Thinking I could help the isolation. Doing something good, but I'm not doing that either. I'm wasting my time on everyone. She doesn't want me there. She doesn't need my help. You don't want me here, you don't want anything from me, but pizza."

I headed toward the door. "I can't keep doing this. I can't keep forcing myself on people, thinking I can make them want me or like me or whatever."

Sam hadn't said a word doing my moment of self-discovery. I'm not even sure if he realized I was in the midst of a breakdown. I left the room, went up the stairs, and right out the door directly to my car. I headed home, my brain still in a flutter of angst.

I arrived home and was greeted by my father, who was seated at the kitchen table. "Good, you're home. I wanted a moment of your time."

"I'm a little busy right now," I said. "Maybe another day. Better yet, make an appointment. I'm not at your beck and call."

"Abigail," he said with a firm authority that I tried to ignore, but I couldn't. I turned from my flight up the steps to find him standing at the table

"What?" I said. Although the word was clipped, I kept my tone cordial. I wanted to keep my swirling feelings and thoughts inside where only I could see they were in a mix and mess of emotions and hurt.

He paused. Whether it was from something he read in my face or in the sound of my voice, he paused. Then he asked, "Were you out at the house today?"

There was no point in lying. "Yes."

"Were you at the house any other time this week?"

I sighed, big and loud and as full of annoyed boredom as I could. "Yes."

"Why?" he asked in the same confused way his wife had earlier in the day.

"Why not?" I said in a non-answer. "Am I not allowed to stop over? Last I knew every time I turned around everyone, you included, has been telling me how rude I am for not stopping in to check on my mother. Yet, I do it, and now I'm getting the third degree asking why. I can't win with you people."

"That's not what I meant," he said.

"Okay, what did you mean?" I snapped.

He hesitated yet again. Why was he treading so carefully around my feelings? He never had before. Why now? "Just, thank you."

Wow, those words had to taste like ash in his mouth. I was in the mood to be nasty, but I was also tired, so I gave a single nod of my head, then went up the stairs to my room. I changed out of my garlic and marinara-scented clothes and went to see if Derek was home yet.

I found him up in his own room. I leaned against the frame of the door and said, "I'm going for a run. You want to come?"

He lifted his head and more accurately his nose up into the air and took in a deep breath. He didn't turn around to face me. He instead took another step or two further away. "When are you leaving for your aunt's?"

I shrugged. "Next week sometime. I figure I have another few days to a week here, then I will go and spend the moon and the rest with her. So? Do you want to come on a run?"

"No."

"No?" I said with such surprise he could not have missed it.

"No."

"Why not?"

"Your scent." That was all he said.

I have to say, it may have only been two words, but I hated them. Had hated them for about two years at that point. The fact all the males in the clans felt it was a nice thing to tell me I smelled ALL THE TIME was not high on my list of happy things. Normal people don't go around saying stuff like that. They just don't.

"Fine," I said and turned with a flip of my hair. I'd go without him. I didn't actually need him to come, and maybe I did rely on him a bit too much, but I had my reasons. One being I didn't want to be corralled again and kidnapped. The Hunterz had every reason to hate me right then. I also didn't like that I felt need for Derek all the time. Need of him to protect me, or whatever. I was a strong, intelligent female shifter. I didn't need anyone.

Want, though, that was another thing altogether. I wanted him to come. I liked the fun of the race. The companionship, even in the silence of the wolf form, was comfortable. I felt calm and easy with him when I ran. But, no, I didn't need him. So, I'd go without him. Fine.

I hit the back door and shifted on the fly as I bounded down the back stairs. My mouth elongated and my teeth pushed back, and the rest was all a blur. Aside from the one moment of awareness, the rest was fast and blank.

I landed on the cool grass and raced across the lawn toward the forest. My muscles stretched and warmed as I ran full out. My paws hit the ground in a one two…three four beat that propelled me with a speed I never could have achieved as a human.

The air was still, but as I ran, a breeze flowed through the fur at my face and chest, allowing me to stay cool even in the hot of the coming July. That was what I needed. The freedom of a run. Everything felt right, felt better as a wolf.

I felt the sadness and tension I'd been carrying ease off. It didn't disappear, but yes, it faded a bit. I made the tree line and without a second of hesitation, leaped right over it. Usually I went to the left, which took me toward town and my mom's house. It wasn't a conscious choice, it had always just been, head left.

That day, I wanted as far away from my mom's house and town as I could get. So, I went right. Had I ever gone the other way before? It felt familiar, but I wasn't sure if I had. Not really. I ran through the forest, around and passed trees. I leapt over fallen branches and logs. I came to a ravine and bounded over it with a strong jump.

I ran for a long while and only stopped when the shadows started to grow long, and the fierce heat of the day felt cooler. Not cool, but less intense. I dropped down into bunch of thick ivy. The leaves were cold on the pads of my feet and the part of my tummy that was not as fur covered as the rest of me.

I settled there and waited for my heart to slow from my trek. The forest was silent around me, which was my first clue all was not grand in the woods. A forest should be teaming with animals and birds. They all had their own sounds. To a human it may seem empty and quiet, but as a wolf, I could smell and hear and see more. I could tell there were animals around me, because of these scenes. I knew they were still there. The fact they were silent and still, was the worry. No birds were screaming out warnings there was a predator in the area. No animals were scurrying out of the way to hide. They were there, but they were frozen and silent, barely breathing.

I didn't move a muscle but for my eyes. I kept them half open, but I was searching around me for the danger. What and where was it? I drew in a long breath, trying to find its scent. It was there, in the air, I just had to understand it. It was a wild scent. Not dirty or rotten, but wild. Maybe a better term was animal like. That didn't mean good or bad. It just meant not human, or not entirely human.

Since I understood all humans were not as they appeared, I took that to mean not all wolves were either. However, the smell of wolves, males, and shifters were all subtly different. A full wolf didn't smell of a human. It only smelled like animal. However, both shifters and some humans smelled like both. Maybe more of one than the other depending on what side was the stronger, but they had both wolf as well as human in them.

That was how I'd found Sam to begin with. He was still a child, but the wolf was rising within him. I could smell it coming off his body through his skin.

The scent I was catching was definitely wolf and it was definitely human. It wasn't one I knew either. I could pick out any shifter I knew in a group of thousands just by their personal scent. The shifter coming my way was a stranger, which meant he was dangerous. I knew most of the shifters in both clans. No, maybe not all of them, but most.

I stayed completely still, as if I was sleeping or resting. Could he tell I was a shifter too? Could he tell I was a girl? I waited for him to come into view. He didn't. I listened but didn't hear any movement. Did he know I was there? Was he just watching me? Could he see me?

All these questions were swirling about in my head and still there was no sign of him other than his scent. I knew he was there. I listened with more concentration. Maybe I could hear him breathing and that would give me an indication of where he was. Nothing. No hint at all.

We played that game of frozen silence for a long time. I say it was a game, as I had come to realize he was waiting for me to move and I was waiting for the same thing. Who would give up first? The shadows changed from long to nonexistent. The sun was down, and the moon was rising. I had been gone a long time.

I couldn't say no one would worry, as I knew my grandfather would, and Derek, although he knew I went for a run, would worry when I didn't return. If I stayed there long enough, someone had to come looking for me. Sooner or later.

I felt my heart hit once a little harder than it had just a second before. It was as I realized, I took a different route that day. How long would it take for Derek to go right, instead of my usual left? I could be there forever. No, he could follow my scent. He'd basically said out loud that my smell was thick and heavy...wait...

The shifter sitting there in wait, he knew I was a girl and he knew I was alone because of my smell. My day just got better and better. I went from being a bit afraid and cautious to getting angry. Enough of the games.

I stood slowly, as if I'd been sleeping. I stretched out my body in as seductive a fashion as I could come up with. I admit I didn't know what I was doing but I figured a bit of body posturing would bring the attention away from me fully and more onto the idea of a girl wolf coming into her fertile period. You know, make the hormones work for me for once, instead of against me.

I walked around in slow circle as if a bit lost and trying to get my bearings. Then I trotted off in the direction of home. I wanted to appear as not threatening as I could. Innocent and naïve was what I was going for.

I made it maybe twenty yards, when I heard movement. I was waiting for it and not distracted by the feel of freedom I'd had at the start. It was a creeping quiet movement, but I heard it all the same. I didn't pick up my pace. I hoped I appeared as unaware and or uncaring as I was trying to be.

After I'd jumped over an old green moss-covered log, I intentionally picked up my pace a bit. Not a lot to seem like I was running from anything in particular, I just sped up. The sound of movement became a bit sloppier, the faster I went. I still didn't see anyone or thing coming up behind me, but I knew they were there, and they were following.

The fur at the back of my neck began to rise when I realized my pursuer was gaining on me. I tried to relax so the aggressive fur wouldn't give me away, but I couldn't seem to help it. My animal instincts were warning me of danger. I prepared to leap over another log, a much bigger and fresher one, when I heard the solid hit of paws to the ground coming up fast behind me.

My pursuer was done playing his game and he was out to pounce. At the last moment before I would have hopped over the wood, I pivoted and leapt to the side. At that same moment, a black and white wolf shot past me and pounced. He missed me by a mile, and instead captured the fallen tree.

I've said before it's a shame, wolves can't laugh as I was inside the form all the same. It came out in a huffy growling sound. Seeing his surprised and shocked face, was so worth it. I wanted to shift just to tell him to step off, but I couldn't do it. I really needed to get over the naked form thing. No one else seemed to mind it.

I turned from the wolf, lifted my tail up with a swish, showing my disdain of him and his antics and again headed home. Sadly, he followed. Did I turn and ask him what he wanted? Did I have to shift and deal with it?

I should have shifted in the forest, that way I could get almost home and just put on my clothes. No, I'd had to in a mood and go wolf at the door, destroying my clothes. I really needed to think ahead a bit. You just never knew when you were going to need clothes. I should start stashing clothes in the forest here and there, for times just like this.

I did a quick glance backward and saw the black and white wolf bearing down on me again. I put on more speed and tried to give myself a little breathing room. He just sped up as well though. I may know these woods pretty well, but this section was not my turf.

He was going to catch me. I needed to be prepared for that. I also needed to figure out what to do when it happened. Then I said to hell with it. I stopped dead, mid-run, and turned to face him. He almost plowed me over. I guess he hadn't been expecting that.

At the last moment he stepped to the side. He blew several steps passed me before coming to a stop. It had been a very close call. I'd felt the breeze brush past my nose, he'd been so close to knocking me down. We stood and stared at one another.

His fur was very shiny. Longer than I'd seen before. It was black, with white chunky sections and spots. The black was heavier in color than the white, except on his face. The fur was in a pattern where the white circled his eyes, ran down his long nose, and ended just over his mouth. It was skull like but striking. His eyes were big, and black. Not brown, full black. His eyes in human form I'd bet were scary and intense, as in the wolf form, they were even more so.

He snarled his jowls over his teeth and emanated a deep growl. I admit it, I was shaking in my fur. I hoped he didn't know how intimidating he was. I had a feeling he knew exactly what I was feeling, but I was hoping all the same.

I sat down, tilted my head, and watched him. He wasn't advancing on me. He wasn't being aggressive other than the noise he was making. I wanted to ask what the hell but wasn't sure how to do that as a wolf. So, I settled on nonchalance. I flopped down in the dirt, dropped my head on my paws and sighed as if bored.

With a frustrated growl, he shifted out of wolf and into his human form. Holy crap on a stick, naked gorgeous man. You'd think I'd be used to naked good-looking guys, thanks to Derek and all the other guys running about in the clans, but it never became boring for me. Woo hoo.

I was not shifting out of my wolf form for anything right then. I knew I was blushing from snout to tail. I could feel my body temperature increase. Yeah, there was no way I was shifting.

Who was he and where did he come from? I didn't think he was part of the Staten clan. Yes, there was variety among the clan, but a good percentage was tall with dark hair and somewhat pale skin. There were many eyes that were different, but the main staple was tall, dark, and handsome. The Grey clan was lighter in hair, but they also were among the tall and handsome.

The shifter that stood before me was not tall; he was just average in height. He was buff and built. I mean, he could put the strong man to shame, he was so bulked up and ripped. His hair was dark, so dark it looked like black ink. It was long, past his shoulders. I couldn't see how far down his back it flowed, but I had a feeling his hair could be as long or maybe longer than my own. His skin was a rich sienna and looked flawless. His eyes were big, seductive big, and matched his hair in darkness. I couldn't tell if they were black or just a really dark brown, but all in all he was gorgeous. Figures.

My eyes followed the contours of his body from his high cheek bones, down his chest, to the little dark trail…ack! I yanked my eyes back to his face. There went my façade of disinterest. He was smiling. He knew exactly what my thoughts where, where my eyes were interested, and that my body temperature was skyrocketing.

"Did you get a good look, little one?" he said with an accent that I would bet money was southern.

I didn't respond to his taunt. Instead, I shifted my body a bit more to the side and turned my head away from him just enough to appear rude.

He laughed instead of being upset. That was interesting. "Come out and talk to me little wolf."

Not happening. I could see from the strength of his body, I would never have been able to outrun him. He didn't appear to be stupid, so I would have to work twice as hard to outwit him.

He crouched down and locked my eyes to his. I admit I allowed it. I wanted to see what he would do or say. He surprised me with his intensity. His eyes were sad eyes. Maybe that is why they looked so big and beautiful. Their emotion pulled me in because I felt the same way…a lot of the time. "I won't hurt you little one. I just want to see you. Maybe talk a bit."

Knowing it could very well be a huge mistake, I decided to shift. No, not right out in the open. I stood, and all the while keeping one eye on him, and his on me, I stepped over to an area that had a bit of cover. Leafy young trees and bushes. I shifted all the while trying to keep a bit of cover over me while I did so. I pulled my wild long hair over my shoulders to use it for coverage of my chest. The leaves and branches I stood behind gave me enough coverage for the lower half of my body to give me a semblance of modesty, at least in my own eyes.

I crossed my arms at my waist and looked him in eye. "This is it," I said. "Nothing spectacular. Nothing exciting. Just me."

A slow appreciative smile lifted the curves of his mouth. "That all depends on the eye of the beholder. You are in fact…spectacular."

I had to turn away from the weight of his stare. I looked out over to the side of him trying to decide what to do or say. I was at the very least way out of my element.

"Who are you?" he asked.

I shrugged my shoulder. "Abby," I said.

"Brinn," he said.

I blinked. Was that his name? What was he trying to say? "Where do you come from?" I asked. I had to know. It was going to drive me crazy. He was so not a Grey or a Staten.

He gave me back the one shoulder shrug and said, "A Cousin."

We were going to get nowhere if we kept at it all night like that. "Okay fine. I need to get home. Why are you following me?"

A big wolfish smile was part of my answer. The rest was, "Your body called to mine. It's still calling to mine."

"My body did no such thing," I snapped.

"You are close to your time, yes?"

I gave him the most disgusted look I could make and said, 'Ew."

He spread his arms wide and replied, "It's all part of nature, little one. You have to appreciate such fine design. I bet you are calling out to wolves for miles and miles. You don't even realize it."

I tried to appear unaffected, but what he said made me a little nervous. Well, more so than I already was. How far could a wolf catch a scent from? "That's not my problem really. You males will just have to get control of yourselves. I, however, can't help it. It's…what did you call it? Natural?"

"We will see how well that idea works for you." He took a deep showy and noisy breath in through his nose. "How far into the cycle are you?"

I was not answering that. Is this what the females had to put up with in the past? No wonder the clan guys were overprotective to the point of trying to keep us prisoners. If Brinn was any indication of the male shifters out there, I was going to have problems out on my own.

"Go home," I said.

I didn't wait for his response. I turned away from him and shifted back to wolf. I was going to make a run for it. I'd either make it or not. I had to try though. I took off with a leap and hit the ground running.

I heard him laugh at my retreating back. He yelled, "Run home, little wolf. I'll see you soon."

Like hell he would. I was going to make sure of it.

Chapter Six

I ran all the way home and directly inside, still in wolf form. I had a small group pacing and stalking the house, waiting for me the second I hit the door.

"Where have you been?" That was Derek. Shocker, he was always the loudest.

"It's late to be coming in. You worried us, Abigail." That was my grandfather.

I nodded at my grandfather to let him know I heard him. I went upstairs to change into human form and to put on some clothes. Before leaving my room, I took a deep breath to prepare myself for the inquisition and went back down to face them.

"I'm sorry I'm late, but Derek knew where I was. I told him I was going for a run. He didn't have time to come with me." I held up my hand as Derek tried to start in on me. "It's too bad you couldn't take some time to come with me as I ran into a stranger. A shifter stranger."

"What? Who?" Derek snapped.

I ignored Derek for a moment and turned on my grandfather. "Are there other clans out there besides us?"

I watched his face very closely. I was getting to know him pretty well, but I couldn't always tell what he was thinking or whether or not he was lying. He had some sixth sense when it came to truth and lies, but I didn't. "There has been talk," he said.

"What?" Derek said with genuine surprise in his tone.

"What kind of talk?" I asked.

I knew I had to ask the questions in order to get the answers. He wasn't about to give anything away on his own.

"Just talk."

"From? With who?" I continued.

"There is a small group of the older generation who believes we are not as…contained here as we like to believe."

"Like Sam," I said.

"Exactly. When you brought Sam into the fold, it became more evident that we were not as alone in the world as we believed. Our girls were kept at home. Wait, I know what you are going to say, but it was a different time, back then. Things are changing now, but back then girls were kept home. The boys, however, were allowed to go out and…shall we say, enjoy being men."

"You mean slut around with any warm body they could find," I said.

"Respect, Abigail," he said with a very evident growl in his tone. He may be old, but he was still a wolf and he was very powerful in his own rights.

"I'm sorry," I said.

He was right. Times were changing. I was part of that change, but I couldn't erase the past. It was what it was and being rude to my grandfather was not a good way to deal with it.

"When you found the boy, the murmurs began again about others out there like us. It's not exactly possible to go out and find them all," he said.

Well, we could, I guess. We would just have to go out with one of our kind who also had a great sense of smell. The problem being that the world was big. It was possible, but not exactly doable and practical.

"However, we are starting to realize there are many others out there who are of our blood."

Derek just stood there with his mouth a bit open in complete disbelief. I wasn't far from the same. All this time I'd thought we were this safe and enclosed little community and it was a lie. Fake walls built on fake security. What did that mean for me? The last female shifter? Well, not last, there was Aunt Lilly of course, but I was the only one in the last…fifty years. Or, was I?

"Tell me about the one you met," my grandfather said, interrupting my thoughts.

I again looked at Derek and we shared a moment of *what the hell*, with each other with nothing but a glance. I turned back to my grandfather and tried to find words to answer his question. "He was not like us."

"What does that mean?" Derek asked.

He was annoyed. I could tell as he jerked out a chair by the table and sat down heavily.

"He was built very different than either of the Greys or Statens. He was big, but not tall. He was huge and built though. I mean HUGE. I could not believe the muscles on the guy. I mean, whoo."

"Okay, he was cut. Can we move on?" Derek snarled.

Jealousy was rearing its head. I smiled and said, "Seriously, you don't have anything to worry about. He was built and buff, but he was so not my type. Just because someone is nice to look at does not mean anything more than that."

"What did he want?" my grandfather asked, getting to the point I had been kind of avoiding, but knowing I would need to get to it all the same, sooner or later. I'd been working on later, but…

"Me," I said.

Derek's response was very feral. He growled low and long, before he said, "Well, he can't have you."

"I was going to wait another week before going to my aunt's, but I think, I should just head out tomorrow. Put a little space between me and the growing crowd of young hormone-filled males."

"That's probably a good idea," my grandfather said.

"I'll go with you," Derek said.

Great, just what I needed, a bodyguard. I so didn't love that.

~ * ~

The next day dawned bright and hot. Summer was coming and the heat of it was showing itself early. I stopped into the pizza place, as soon as they opened to tell them I would be out of town for a week or so.

"That's not how vacation time works," Tammy said. "You have to put in a request, and have it approved, then you can take a vacation. As it is, you aren't approved. Therefore, I expect you to be at work."

I was not a fan of Tammy, at all. However, I did see her point, even if I didn't want to admit it. I didn't have a choice though. I couldn't stay in town as I was. "I'm sorry Tammy, I will not be in. I have to go to my aunt's. I don't have a choice."

I should have realized what was coming as she smiled. It was gleeful and happy. "Well then, I don't have a choice either," she said. "You're fired."

"Seriously?" I replied.

"Your final paycheck will be mailed to you," she said.

My only paycheck. Just great. Being a girl shifter was not fair.

I drove directly from the pizza place out to my aunt's home. Derek would come out in the evening after work as well. He wouldn't have any trouble taking off to be with me. Oh no. He definitely wouldn't be fired for it. I really hated to admit it, but I guess there was a perk to working for the family businesses.

I pulled into the driveway of my aunt's and before I could get all the way out of the car, I was swarmed by her pack of dogs. They all had names, but I could never keep them straight. Plus, there were so many that came and went at will, I was never sure who was there and who wasn't. "Get down, get down." I was laughing and trying to get the weight of the happy animals off me, all the while trying to get to the porch.

A sharp whistle dropped them all to the ground instantly. They then took off at a run to surround my aunt. "How do you do that?" I asked.

"Practice, lots and lots of practice." She wrapped me in a warm hug and said, "It's good to see you. Where have you been?"

"School, life, you know," I said.

"Yes, I do." We made our way to the chairs lining part of the porch. After we were settled in our seats and the dogs had laid down and quieted, she said, "So, tell me the news of your part of the world."

"News of my world, well, it sucks to be a girl."

She laughed. She threw her head back and laughed. Her long silver-white hair was in a messy bun on top of her head and her blue eyes were squinted against the sun. She was lovely. I could only hope to age as well as her. "Yes, it does sometimes," she said. "What's going on?"

"How did you survive your 'P' when you were my age? I mean, for real. This is stupid." I said.

"Oh, it was tough. It's one of the reasons we mate so young. It helps. It's not fair and it's not easy, but it helps to be mated."

"Ugh, that is not going to happen. What if I go on birth control? The kind that makes it so you don't have a period. Maybe that would help."

She only laughed again. "You know birth control doesn't work on us, right?"

I made a face and said, "No. I didn't. That would have been good knowledge to have."

"Your best bet is to just stay low during your time."

"I can't just stay in a basement for weeks and wait for it to be over. I have, well, I had a job. I have things to do. I can't just go into hiding every six months for a month. This is the twenty-first century. There has to be a better way."

She shook her head and said, "None that I can think of right now."

"How am I supposed to go to college and work? How will I have my own life?"

It wasn't fair. I was going to be trapped in the shifter world. Working where they said. Living where they said. Doing what they said. All because males couldn't control themselves when I was fertile.

"Don't take it so hard. It's only twice a year and it really does go quick. Once you get used to it, you kind of learn to go with the flow. Don't make it such a big deal. It's really not."

It was to me.

"Tell me what else is new," she said, changing the subject.

"Well, a new male was found. Not from either of our clans."

"I already know about Sam, remember? I was there."

"No, not Sam. A different guy."

She sat up and paid attention then. "From where? What kind of guy?"

"I don't know where he came from and I don't know what you mean by kind of guy? He was a guy, guy."

"No, tell me what he looked like. How do you know he was different?"

"Well, his skin isn't as pale as ours. His eyes are really dark. He's tall, but not as tall as our guys. He's big, though. I mean, like, huge."

"Oo la, so he's hot?"

I turned wide surprised eyes on her. "Are you serious?"

"I may be old, but I'm not dead. I can still appreciate a pretty face and body."

"Ew," I said, but it made me laugh all the same. "Yes, he was hot. He was kind of scary too though, so it took away from his pretty face."

"How did you find him?"

"Well...I didn't. He found me. Said he'd come from far away for me. He...sensed me."

"Oh."

I think she finally realized why I was not happy about being a girl. "Things were not like that in my younger days. People didn't go around talking about it. Girls just went into a sort of confinement. After they were hidden away for a period, they simply returned to life. There wasn't any big deal made. However, if males were coming in from all over the place, I can see why it's a little disconcerting."

"To say the least. Not a fan," I said.

"Well, I guess we will have to put our heads together and figure out a better way to deal with the situation."

"Well, I have at least two more weeks here, so we should be able to come up with an idea or two. You sure you don't mind me staying that long?"

"Are you kidding? Honey, you have your own room here for a reason. I love having you. I mean it. You are a joy to me."

She laid a hand on my arm and made sure I was looking at her as she said it.

Why couldn't my mom be like her? I wished, not for the first time, that she was my mom. Not that it would do me any good. Wishes were just that. Nothing. "Thank you. I didn't know where to go where I would also want to be. Thank you for always taking me in."

"Anytime. I mean it. Any time at all." She sat back in her chair and began to gently rock. "Tell me how Sam is doing."

"Ugh, that is not going well either. He won't even look at me, let along talk to me. I'm getting nowhere."

"Don't worry. I think that will just take patience and time."

"I hope. Not that these two weeks away will do me any good with him. Maybe he and I can both see it as a reprieve from the uncomfortable silence of our visits."

"That's one way to look at it."

"Hey, the full moon is this week, too. We can enjoy that together, too. Another month of you not having to hide. How does it feel to be one of the balanced?"

"You ask me the same thing every month. It feels fine. There isn't much difference. Aside from not being controlled by the animal side of my genes, it's the same."

"I guess," I said.

It was a bit of a letdown to be honest. I'd been hoping for something more. Some grand change and feel to being balanced versus unbalanced.

"Don't get me wrong, it's great to be balanced. Having more control over ourselves was a huge relief to us both. We now work together, and we aren't fighting for dominance over the other all the time. We are both just me now. You know what I mean?"

"I do." I said. "Maybe being balanced as a male is more dramatic?"

"What do you mean?

"Well, it just seems like nothing all that exciting for you. I thought it was going to be one of those great wonderful things. Everything would be grand in the world, but it's not any different."

"It is different. Maybe you are right though, and the males will be more. They are more controlled by the wolf. I wasn't. I never was. She was more of a friend to me. Someone I could hide behind when I needed to. I was never fighting her to stay inside. Well, except at the full moon, but that was all. The males fight their wolves for dominance all the time, every day. It's different for them. We fight our hormones, but they fight themselves. I guess they have their own unfair kind of things.

We both rocked in our chairs. I don't know what she was thinking, but I was thinking how it must not feel fair to the males either. I hadn't seen the other side.

The rest of our time together was easy. Derek came that night and stayed with us to make sure we weren't followed. I say we, but we all knew we were talking about me. I was the one putting out a beacon for others to follow.

The night of the full moon came and went without issue. Derek went out and ran the forest most of the night. I stayed in. I was too close to be out with the wolves when they had more control than the humans.

The day after the full moon dawned. I couldn't sleep. I felt…off. Derek dragged himself to the kitchen. "You look like crap," I said.

"You should talk," he said.

He pulled a cup down and poured himself some coffee. He took one sip then slammed the cup down the counter so hard, and so suddenly, I am surprised it didn't break. I, however, just about jumped out of my skin.

"What is wrong with you?" I snapped.

It was way too early for his drama.

"You!" he said or more like growled at me.

"I am not doing anything," I snapped right back at him. "I'm sitting here."

"God, you have no idea what it's like. Can't you at least shower or something? You're killing me."

"Screw you," I said.

Before I could get good and mad, he left the kitchen in a huff and went outside, leaving his coffee on the counter.

"Jerk," I said, but it was more under my breath than anything.

"I see the morning is going well," my aunt said from where she stood in the doorway from the hall.

"He's in a mood," I said.

"It's not just him. You're cranky, too."

"I know," I said.

I did. I could feel the mood coursing through my system. I was mad, I was sad, I was annoyed, but there wasn't any reason for it. "You know, I thought being a wolf and going into heat would feel more…I don't know, sexy or something. I just feel like I have serious PMS."

Aunt Lilly laughed. "Oh, you are too much."

"I'm serious," I said.

After pouring herself a cup of coffee she sat down across the table from me. "Have you shifted to wolf lately?"

I shrugged. "No."

There hadn't been any reason too and I hadn't felt like it.

"This is your second cycle, right?"

"Yeah."

"Did you shift during that one?"

"No. Why?"

"Well, from my experience, and this is only mine, you could have a different one, but the wolf is the one in heat, not you the human. So, you don't feel the effects of it as you would in the wolf form. Now, before you run out to shift, I suggest you wait until you are in a mated, preferably married couple, before you try it out. It can be...intense."

I sat there thinking it out. "So, now that you've told me it's some crazy intense thing to be a wolf while I'm dealing with this, you want me to not go try it out? You do know that is right up there with, don't look down. I kind of need to look now."

She shrugged one dainty shoulder and said, "Just remember, I warned you."

"What exactly will I feel?"

"I don't know. I only know what I felt. You are balanced, maybe you won't feel anything different. I would suggest you don't shift anywhere near Derek. That is not fair to him. He's struggling as it is."

I didn't race right out and shift. I was too tired. The not sleeping was catching up with me. I showered and got dressed in as little as possible. My skin was all itchy and sensitive, so I put on yoga pants and a loose tank. My hair was heavy on my head, but it felt better to be loose and free than it did to try to pull it back. I found my aunt in her yellow room. That really was a great room, but that day it didn't calm me like it normally did. "I think I'm going to go for a walk. I feel antsy."

She looked me over and said, "You want company?"

She was enjoying a book. There was a cup of tea sitting on the little table. I could tell she was happy where she was but would drop it all and come with me if I asked. I didn't want her to do that. So, I said, "Nah, I'm not great company right now. I'll be back soon. I just want to work off some of this weird energy."

"I know what you mean."

I bet she did. As one of the few shifter females, she had more experience than I did. I stepped out of the cool house and the blast of hot air hit me full on. I almost went back inside. Almost. A small group of dogs were laying in a pile on the porch. Even they weren't enjoying the heat. Aside from one lifting its head in greeting, they barely moved when I walked past them and headed toward the forest.

I stepped into the shade of the trees. It didn't help all that much, but it did help. I took maybe five steps inside when the hairs on the back of my neck stood up. Instantly alert, I still was not prepared to be pounced on from behind.

At first, I thought it was Derek and I started to laugh thinking he was playing, but then the smell hit me. It was wilder and deeper and not Derek. I hit the ground almost face first. I caught myself as best I could with my arms and hands. I felt the forest debris slice and poke into my skin. I was going to pay for that for a day or so. Fast healing or not, it still hurt.

Before I could really do more than register it was Brinn, and he'd found me, I was flipped over to face him. He was not more than an inch away from my nose and he was breathing right on me. His hand circled my neck. I felt his thumb running over my pulse, where I am sure it was beating hard and fast.

"I found you," he said almost on a whisper. "I told you, you'd see me soon, little one."

His large heavy body pressed my smaller one down into the dirt. He was intentionally using his weight against me. The ground was sticking me in the back where my skin was bare. Plus, my shirt had ridden up in the back exposing more of skin to the ground more readily than it would have otherwise. At least I wasn't wearing shorts. My legs would have taken a beating as well.

I tried to struggle under his weight. I didn't go anywhere, and I could tell he could see it in my face that I was on the verge of panic. He smiled. The jerk had the gall to smile in my face while I was suffocating under his behemoth body. "I can't breathe," I gasped.

"Sure you can. If you can talk, you can breathe."

I began to struggle in earnest, as I wasn't lying. I really couldn't get a good breath with him pressing down on my lungs. Thankfully, he eased up off me just enough to let me take a full and deep breath. That did several things in my favor. One, it allowed me to calm my racing fear and two, it allowed me to think of something other than suffocating. Something like how to get out of the situation I was in.

"What do you want?" I said. It wasn't as snappish as you'd think it would be, considering the circumstance. It was a genuine enquiry.

"You know what I want." To prove his point, he ran one hand up my leg and landed at my waist. His hand was big and wrapped from my hip bone around to the side. He smelled thick and suffocating and his body was sweating and hot against mine.

"Don't," I said and tried to grab his hand and pull it off my body.

"You have no idea what you are doing to me, do you? You are so sweet and innocent. I want you. Right now," he said and dropped his mouth onto mine.

I pressed my lips as tightly closed as I could and squealed a sound of distress he didn't seem to care about. He shoved his thick and wet tongue in my mouth and almost down my throat.

I gagged. Then I got mad. I clamped my teeth down on his tongue with enough force I tasted blood. He yanked away from me with a grunt, and I turned my head away from him with a forceful jerk. "Bitch," he snarled.

I was furious. I laughed in his face and said, "I'm the bitch? You push your disgusting tongue in my mouth without my permission, just force it down my throat and you call me a bitch?"

He grabbed my shoulders, pulled me up and then slammed me back down against the ground once to make his point. "You are going to regret that."

The blood in my mouth, I tried to spit in his face, but part of me, the part that I wasn't always proud of, swallowed it down with an appetite for more. That was not a good sign. My vision was turning from clear and pinpoint to blurry red around the edges.

I snarled in warning to him, as well as to myself. I tried to push back the shift to wolf, but blood was one of those things that tended to make me lose all control and bring the animal part forward whether my brain wanted it to or not. I began to fight him, and he began to struggle. Where before it had been fun for him, as he felt he was in charge. Bigger, stronger. As my wolf came forward with blood on its mind, it wasn't fun anymore.

My jaw cracked and extended. My back arched, pushing him up. That should have been warning enough I was losing control. He was apparently thick and didn't see the danger heading his way. After that point, I didn't try to fight the shift. I could tell it was inevitable. I let go and allowed the wolf to come. She came and several things hit me at once.

One, his smell was very different to me in wolf form than it had been as a human. Where it had been thick and gross, it was now tantalizing and although hard to admit, also mouthwatering. My body felt alive and the feel of his big body against it, felt awesome.

Inside, I tried to find the ew factor, I had had before, but all I could sense was how fine a male he was. I stopped fighting the same moment he did as well. He shifted to meet me as a wolf instead of a man and that was a huge mistake on both our human parts.

Me, as a wolf, I was out of control. Along with the blood lust coursing through me, I also had a very basic need running alongside the other. I rolled to my feet and met him nose to nose. I stepped in close to him and ran my long body against his. When I reached his tail, I turned around and gave the same treatment to the other side. The feel of his warmth and his fur made my blood race more than it had been.

I ran my face against his neck and muzzle. I was learning his smell and his contours. I didn't know what I was doing, only that my instincts were taking over, and I was letting them. I hesitated a moment. I knew it was wrong, but it didn't feel wrong.

He sensed my hesitation, and when I stepped back to give myself some breathing room, he crowded in close to take it away. He knew, I don't know how he knew, but he knew, I was trying to regain some semblance of control of my wayward hormones. I could tell he didn't want that to happen. He wanted the animal DNA in control, not the human one.

Before I lost all sense of myself to the needs of my wolf, I forced myself to push back the blood and shifted back to human. I saw Brinn's intent and as he pounced on me, I screamed as loud as I could, before the air was shoved out of me when I hit the ground and his weight hit my chest.

I was naked and completely at his mercy. I was in big trouble. I couldn't use my wolf to help as the animal side of me was just as out of control as he was. I took in another breath and screamed again. I had to get Derek's attention. Where was he?

It wasn't that I needed a man to save me, it wasn't. Right then, though, I could use the help.

Brinn shifted and we were both bare. Our bodies pressed skin to skin. I was not in the least bit turned on by this, he, however…really was. Fear like no other hit me full force. "No," I whispered.

"It's too late, little one. I can't help it now," he said. He pushed my struggling shoulders down to the ground to try to stop my struggles. "I didn't want it to be this way, but…"

I took a deep breath to try to scream again, and that was when it hit me. Derek. I turned my head just in time to see the dark wolf come barreling through the trees. He didn't hesitate. He didn't faulter. He hit Brinn full force in his chest and stomach, toppling him backward over and off me to land in an awkward heap. Derek trampled right over top of him, then turned and came back for more. His jowls were pulled back and his teeth were bared and then he snapped. He didn't give a second before he attacked. Teeth dug into thick muscle. Blood spurted and fell to the dirt, turning it to red mud. I rolled away. I crawled up to my knees. I forced myself, fought my way to my feet.

I didn't want to stay and watch. I was afraid. Really afraid right then. More than I had been when I'd thought I was dead at the hands of the Hunterz. I'd been ready for that, mentally at least. I'd spent days preparing to either escape or die. I was not prepared to be raped in the woods or to watch Derek tear Brinn apart. I had to get away before the smell of blood overwhelmed me again and I lost control.

I ran. I ran hard and fast. I ran to the house and inside. I stumbled my way down to the little basement where my aunt had hidden for years during the full moon. I closed and locked the door. I hid naked and afraid in the plush little room. I didn't know I was whimpering and crying until the sound started to grate on my nerves.

I quieted. I calmed down enough for my heart to not feel like it was going to beat out of my chest. After I settled even more, I found my bearings and looked around the room. I'd been in there before. Aunt Lilly had spent many full moons in there hiding away, pretending she wasn't able to shift anymore in order to gain or keep her freedom.

Now, I was there hiding in the same space. I didn't understand what happened. How I arrived at that place. All I'd wanted was a bit of quiet. A moment of space. What I received was being attacked, pawed at, blood, and violence. I began to cry again, while I pulled out a pair of leggings and a long t-shirt from the dresser.

The room was stocked with clothes and had a small half bath. The only thing lacking was food. There was a soft knock at the door. I didn't want to respond, but I figured by the gentleness of the rap, it was not Derek or Brinn for that matter. I padded over to the door on bare feet and opened the door just enough to see out.

My aunt stood there with a cup of tea and a sad smile. "It's going to be all right."

I began to cry again, as I let her in the space with me. "How? How is this all right?"

She petted me as we walked over to the small couch. We sat down together, and I curled into her for comfort. She didn't shy away from me, in fact she pulled me closer and rested her chin on my head. "It will get easier. You'll find your own rhythm and ways of handling this. You'll see. It won't always be this hard."

"Is Derek okay?" I sniffed and tried to dry my eyes, but the tears just kept coming.

"He's fine. Once you were out of direct contact, calmer minds were able to be found."

"So, this is my fault too," I wailed and started crying all the more. "Why are you laughing? This isn't funny."

"No, it's not. I just remember feeling almost the exact same way when I was your age. It's not fair, is it?"

"No."

"Well, know this. It's not your fault. No, it's not," she said when I started to interrupt. "I know it feels like it, but this is going to pass, and the next time, will be better."

"I'm just going to live down here forever," I said petulantly.

"Well, you are welcome to come and stay anytime, but you can't live down here. You can use it when you feel overwhelmed, or when it seems like the world is closing in. However, you can't hide away in here forever. It's not our way. We Staton girls are made of tougher stuff than that. Once you have had a bit of time to process, you'll see. You are more than this."

"Okay." It was as much as I could give at that point. It was enough though. Aunt Lilly gave my shoulders another squeeze, then after disentangling herself from my cling, she stood up. "Drink your tea. Rest and relax down here. Stay as long as you want, but you have to come up for meals. Deal?"

I thought it over and realized it was a good offer. "Deal. I think a nap will do me good. I'll see you at dinner."

She started to leave when a thought hit me, "Wait! What happened to Brinn?"

She gave me a crooked smile and said, "I'll let Derek tell you about that one. I think he will enjoy the story."

It must not have been too bad, or she would have just told me. I could deal with that. After she left, I drank the strawberry tea she'd given me. I did as she suggested and had a nap. I really needed it. For once, in what felt like a long time, I slept. When I woke up, I was all disoriented. What time was it?

I hoped it was time to eat as I was suddenly starving. I made a quick stop in the restroom, then slipped quietly out of the room. I tiptoed my way up the stairs. I slowly peeked out around the corner. The aroma of fried chicken hit my senses and I closed my eyes to appreciate it. My mouth watered. I stopped tiptoeing around and went directly to the kitchen to see how long I would have to wait.

Derek was seated at the table. His profiled was toward me, but I could sense him wince as I walked in. I backed up a step. Then I stopped. I lifted my chin and walked the rest of the way in the room. "What?" I barked.

"You have no idea how hard this is. My wolf is literally clawing at me every moment of the day now. He wants out. He thinks he's already mated to your wolf. He doesn't understand why I won't let him have her."

He was right, I didn't have any idea. "I'm sorry."

It wasn't my fault. I was going to take Aunt Lilly's word on that, and just go with it, but I still felt bad for the trouble. He dropped his head to the table. "I don't know if I can make it. I'm going a little crazy here."

I didn't know what to say. "I don't want you to go."

"I don't want to go, but I'm afraid of what I might do if I stay."

"I trust you, Derek."

He shook his head. "Don't. I don't trust myself right now."

The fact he admitted to being almost out of control, gave me seriously pause. I was being selfish by asking him to stay. I would accept whatever he chose to do at that point. I owed that to him after all he did for me. He deserved my understanding. "Okay," I said. "If you do go though, please say goodbye before you do."

I changed the subject then. "What happened with Brinn?"

That garnered a smile out of him. "Let's just say I knocked some control back into him." He didn't elaborate but I got the picture. His face turned thoughtful and he said, "You know, I'm not sure he's really a bad guy."

"Excuse me?" I said.

I tried to hold on to my temper, as Derek was thinking out loud. He was sharing his thoughts with me. I didn't want to shut him down exactly, except for the fact that what he was saying was stupid. "You weren't there."

"No, I wasn't, but I was there after. Once you were out of direct sight, he was able to gain some semblance of sanity back. He looked almost horrified when he did. That tells me he has no training and he is a little out of his element. We know next to nothing about him. Is he alone? Is he part of a wolf clan? Has he ever been around a full shifter female? I don't know any of this stuff." He stared hard at me as he tried to make his point. "Do you?"

"No," I admitted ruefully. I didn't know anything about him either.

"I don't think he's part of a clan. He seems a bit lost."

"He doesn't seem lost to me. He seems out of control and that's not the same thing."

"No, it's not, but think about how you felt when you were changing and had no one to help or explain or just confirm you weren't losing your mind. That's how he seems to me. He's treading water and staying afloat on his own, but he's out in the middle of the ocean, alone and flailing. I want to help him."

"What?" I growled and stood up to tower over him.

He reared back. For a second, I thought I'd scared him, but then I saw his eyes. They dilated. He stood and turned away from me. He put some space between us, then settled to lean against the countertops by the door.

"Why is that so strange? You want to do the same thing for Sam. Why is Brinn any different? If he's out there alone in the world, he needs guidance and a friend the same as Sam does."

"Because! He's not a little boy. He's a...a man."

"So, what? A man doesn't need friends and support?"

"You're twisting my words. Why does it have to be you? It could be anyone else. Someone not as close to me." He didn't know what almost happened out there in the forest. I couldn't, no, I wouldn't forget it. I wouldn't be a part of that friendship. "Just...no."

"You don't want me to tell you what to do, so why would you think it would be okay to do it to me?" he said. There was an evident snarl in his tone.

I didn't care. I was mad he would even suggest it. "Because this has to do with me. I am not going to be a part of this. You aren't either."

He turned away from me again, put both hands against the counter. I saw his entire body clench. "You need to settle down a bit," he said, which made me all the madder.

He knew it too as he tried to explain. "You get angry and your body reacts with adrenalin and hormones. I'm drowning in it."

"So, this is my fault too?" I didn't care how hungry I was, I was done arguing with him. "Do what you want, but I won't be a party to it. Do it somewhere else. Just go." I then left the kitchen empty handed and with an empty stomach. I went back down to the little quiet room and called it a day.

Chapter Seven

I slept like crap. Again. However, I was feeling…better. Not as edgy. There wasn't a simmering anger running through my body. I used the little bathroom to freshen up. That was when I figured out why I was suddenly feeling more like myself. My usual self. Relief caused my knees to weaken and the tight muscles in my entire body to finally relax. I hadn't realized I'd been so tense. I had never in my life been so happy to have a period.

"I wonder when menopause will hit."

I left the room and went upstairs to shower, get dressed. After that I would go find some food. I was absolutely starving. I could eat a whole cow, and as a mostly vegetarian, that said something. "Where's Derek?" I asked when I saw only my aunt sitting in the kitchen.

I didn't stop to sit down though. I went right to making eggs and toast. As I was rooting around in the freezer for bacon or sausage, my aunt said, "He left late last night. He said he'd be back in a week or so."

I spun around to stare at her, then said feebly, "But he didn't say goodbye. He said he wouldn't leave without saying goodbye."

She took a sip from her cup, most likely filled with tea. She was buying time. I could see it in her face as she was trying to find the right words. "I am sorry. I would assume after the screaming match between the two of you, he felt it best to just go."

There was a twinge of reprimand in her tone. It hit hard, maybe because it was given with a gentle hand and not crammed in my face like it normally was by everyone else. My shoulders hunched in shame. "I'm sorry we were so loud. I don't know why I was so angry. I couldn't help it."

"Anger itself isn't a bad thing," she said, again sipping on her tea. "You let it get the best of you, though, and you took out your feelings on Derek. He's a good boy."

He was not a boy anymore. He was a man, but she was right. "I know, but it was more than that. I couldn't contain my feelings. Nothing he said or did would have made any difference then. I couldn't hear anything he had to say over the raging thoughts in my head. It wasn't fair to him. I'll apologize."

She nodded once then let the discussion go. She was so unlike the rest of the family. She said what she had to say and then she would move on. My father, my grandfather, and even Derek felt like they had to drum into my brain what they thought I needed to know or do or be. I turned back to the freezer, feeling a bit better about the situation. I found some bacon and went back to making myself something to eat.

As I was trying to not scarf down my food like an animal, I said, "I will probably be leaving in a few days. I'm feeling better today."

It sounded as if I had been sick. Why I couldn't just come out and say what I wanted to say, I have no idea, but it was as direct as I got to saying I was in the clear for another six to eight months.

The next week passed quickly. I'd left a message on Derek's voicemail, telling him I would be coming home in a few days. I didn't say anything else at that point. I didn't want to say I was sorry on his voicemail. He deserved to be face-to-face with me. Thankfully, we had come out to my aunt's house separately, otherwise I would have been stranded. Having to ask him to come and get me was too hard of a pill to swallow right then.

Pride is not a great thing. Sadly, I seemed to have it in spades. Yes, I hadn't been super supportive and nice to him there at the end. It wasn't exactly my fault either. He could blame and be mad at biology, but not me. I wasn't going to ask him for anything, though. Not until we were on equal footing again.

Without a lot of fuss, I said my goodbyes, and headed home. I did promise to stop back over around my birthday. I hadn't realized until that moment my birthday was only about three weeks away. She wanted to celebrate with me as well but didn't want to impose on any other plans I might have. I didn't have the heart to tell her no one else had plans to celebrate my birthday that I was aware of. I figured it would upset her, and I didn't want to leave with her upset. So, I said I'd be back soon, and I'd call to confirm as we got closer.

I arrived home to a relatively empty house. It was a bit of a letdown. I'd been gone about two weeks. I hadn't seen or heard from Derek in days. As I carried my things up to my room, I tried not to feel sorry for myself, but I did. I had gone from a home where I was a bit spoiled with attention to a home where no one cared if I was there or gone. "Welcome home, Abby. We missed you," I said to the empty room.

I dropped onto the edge of my bed and sighed. Now what? I decided I'd had enough of waiting for other people. I grabbed my keys and headed right back out the door to the little ranch house and Sam.

I walked right in, gave a hello to a somewhat surprised Tanner, and headed directly down the stairs. I had been MIA for a while, so I guess I should have expected everyone else's surprise at my sudden reappearance. Sam's room came into view and I was happy to see there were a few changes. More homey touches to the place. Less neatness and order and more dirt and clutter.

Sam was just standing in the center of the room when I came into view. "I see I was unexpected by the look on your face." I gave him a smile and plopped myself down on the futon. "So, I've decided you are as ready as you are going to get. It's time to start talking about what and who you are."

The only response I received was silence and pair of angry eyes staring me down. Good, at least he was listening.

"You are a shifter."

I didn't sugarcoat it. I just dropped it onto him like a bag of beans.

"Sure I am," he said. Then he changed direction. He walked over to turn on the game station.

I stood up, unplugged it and said, "Nope. Not today. Today, you get to listen, whether you want to or not."

"Fine," he said.

He crossed his arms over his chest and continued to stare angrily at me.

For some reason it didn't bother me. I suppose it's because he had the right to be mad. I'd be mad in his shoes. "You really are a shifter. I think there is even a little piece of you that knows it."

A small glimmer of something, maybe interest lit in his eyes.

"Your brother?" Here I hesitated as I was certain the subject of his brother was going to be touchy. "I think he had a little bit of shifter in him as well. Not as much as you. He would never have been able to shift to a wolf, but he would have had better hearing, sight, and sense of smell. He would have been faster than a regular person and would have maybe had trouble controlling emotions."

I was watching Sam's face carefully for any signs of acknowledgement. I saw a spark of one. "He did, didn't he?"

He didn't agree or disagree, he continued to stand there, pretending he wasn't interested, but he was. He really was.

"Fine," I said and continued. "You on the other hand, I think you have a wolf inside you. I think he will come out soon. You need to be prepared for the changes. It's more than just physical. It's emotional and it's biological. It's not an easy change."

Nothing. No response at all.

"Look, I want to help you. You can accept it or not, but I'm trying here. I know you don't understand. I know you're angry, but I really am trying to be your friend." Still nothing. "Even though you tried to kill me and my family." That part I said to get a reaction. It worked.

"So, what? You killed mine!" he suddenly shrieked in this high-pitched voice filled with pain, as well as rage.

I was prepared for the anger. I was not prepared for the pounce of his surprisingly heavy little body. He weighed more than I expected. When he landed on my chest, I couldn't brace for the hit, and we both toppled down to the floor with a loud thud.

He then began to whale on me with his fists of fury. They struck my chest and my jaw and my shoulders. They were fierce and angry, but they really weren't all that damaging. They hurt, yes, but not so much I couldn't take it. I tried and missed grabbing his hands to halt the assault. I made another grab and was able to close my hands over his wrists. He sat straddled on my stomach. I held his hands up and away from me. We both panted as we stared into each other eyes.

The sound of running heavy steps drew our attention to the stairs. Tanner flew down the steps and stopped. He took in our position but didn't move forward. He obviously had no idea what to do. The situation appeared to be under some control, but was it? Sam was sitting on me and I did have his hands tightly in my own, so he couldn't strike out. I'm sure we looked interesting though.

"Um..." That was the extent of his conversation.

I looked from Tanner to Sam and Sam looked at me. I felt a smile crack over my face, at the same moment Sam burst out laughing. We laughed like loons for a moment, or maybe a bit longer. It wouldn't have lasted as long as it did, but every time we started to get it together, one of us would look at Tanner and his incredulous face and we'd start all over again.

Finally, we sat up. I wiped at the errant tears that were tracking over my face. "Sorry, we were having a moment," I said to Tanner.

He looked from me to Sam on more time, then without any word at all, turned and walked back upstairs. I'm certain he thought we were crazy.

I turned back to Sam and saw he was looking at me. "What?" I asked.

"You seem different today."

"I haven't been feeling all that like myself the last few weeks."

He stood up and brushed off his pants. He seemed awkward and nervous, before he said, "You were gone. I didn't think you were coming back."

I felt bad. I'd been mad at him the last time I saw him, and he'd thought I left him for good. At the time, I'd wanted to go and never look back. That was me just being mad though. "I'm sorry. I went out to visit with my aunt. I needed a break from the world."

"Are you feeling better now?"

That garnered another smile from me. "Yes. Finally."

We sat quietly a moment. I could tell he had things on his mind, but I didn't push. He'd share when he was ready. It was sooner than I expected, as not a few minutes later, he asked, "How do you know I will change into a wolf?"

"You may not know this, but I haven't been a shifter all that long either. I'm still learning my way through a lot of stuff. One of them is the extreme sense of smell we all have. I can sense the wolf inside you. I can smell him in there."

He didn't seem grossed out by it. In fact, he seemed excited. "What does he smell like?"

I shrugged once and said, "It's hard to explain. It's just different. Thicker, maybe? Have you noticed smells more than usual?"

"Maybe," he said, and he looked up like he was thinking really hard. "I thought you smelled gross the last few times you were here, but you don't today, so maybe not."

I wasn't going there with him. He could figure out girls and hormones and fertility all by himself. "What about sight and sound?"

"I don't think I see any better, but I can hear better. I know the sound of your car, so I know when it's you coming in the house. I can also hear Tanner. He likes to sing up there. He has a thing for movie songs."

"Show tunes?" I asked and had to stifle a laugh. The idea of the big muscled Tanner belting out show tunes was almost too much for me.

He shrugged. "I guess. Songs I know from movies."

"That's awesome," I said and couldn't contain a short burst of laughter.

"I'd say you are getting there then. If your skin starts to feel itchy, you need to let someone know."

"Why?"

"Well, I had trouble with my sight first, then sounds, and smells. The itchy skin though about drove me nuts. I didn't have any one to explain it to me. That is a sign you are close to changing. If the full moon is close, I'd say that would be when you shift."

"Are we werewolves? Like in the movies?"

"No, not really. The full moon will make you shift for a while."

"Just me? So, I'll grow out of it?"

"No, well, maybe. I sat down and got comfortable on the futon and said. "Let me tell you a story about magic."

From there I spent the next hour explaining and fielding questions about the gypsy curse. How I broke it for myself. How each shifter would have to find a way to break it for themselves.

"Maybe you will be another of the smart ones to figure it out," I said and gave him a wink.

"I doubt it. No one else has yet," he said.

"Yeah, but you weren't raised in the shifter clans and environment. You are like me. We came into the world without all the shifter rules and notions. You might be able to break free of the so-called curse and find your balance. That's be awesome. You could be the first boy shifter to do it."

He smiled at that.

I glanced at the time and saw it was late. Really late. "I better get going," I said.

Sam jumped to his feet and said in almost a panic. "When will you come back?"

We'd made a lot of headway that day. It was amazing how far we'd come. "I'll come back tomorrow. I promise."

"Will you bring pizza?" he asked a bit sheepishly. "It's not that I expect it," he rushed to say. "It's just that...well, Tanner can't cook very good."

"Sorry buddy, I don't think I can bring pizza. I was fired. I'll find something else to bring along though. How's that?"

"Anything's better than another egg sandwich and tomatoes. I swear that's all we eat around here."

"Okay. I'll see you tomorrow then." I went upstairs and found Tanner.

"Dude, you do realize that's a growing boy down there and you have to feed him more than eggs, right?"

"I'm not a cook," he said not even bothering to look at me.

I stepped into his line of vision and said, "I don't care. Figure something out then. Order in. Get takeout. Do something."

"I'm not a cook," he said again as if I simply didn't hear him the first time.

I grabbed ahold of the neck of his shirt and pulled his attention directly on my face and said, "Tanner, he's a little boy. He's all alone here. Show a little compassion."

His face, usually a mask of nothing, winced at my words. That was good enough for me.

I didn't wait for his reply. I simply went out to my car and went home. Who knew what awaited me there?

It was as expected when I arrived home. Derek and my grandfather were waiting for me in the kitchen. "You know, there is a great big house behind you. You don't have to sit right here by the door all the time," I said.

Derek stood up and with a frown and a growl said, "You know, there is a device that allows you to stay in contact with the people who worry about you. It even fits in your pocket and is travel size. It's called a cell phone."

I shrugged, "I didn't think anyone bothered to care." I was able to pull off the bored uncaring tone, but my face wasn't quite as unaffected. "And I did call. I left a message for you, telling you'd I'd be home."

"You were not exactly expected. You didn't give us a time. We can't wait around all day for you. We have things that must get done. We have jobs."

Usually, that would have set me off. I did have a job until being a stupid girl made that impossible. That day though, I was feeling so much better with my life. I mean, I'd made progress, actual progress, with Sam. I wasn't going to allow Derek to ruin that. "Fine, whatever," I said and decided I wasn't in the mood to spar with him.

"Wait," my grandfather said. "I would like a word with you."

I stopped with one foot on the stairs. I'd been so close to freedom. I pasted a smile on my face and turned to face him. "Sure, what's up?"

"This is a little delicate, and I understand you have many reservations about the process, but after this last…ah…moon of yours, I…we, your father and I, think a formal and complete mating would be a good idea."

"Are you serious?" I asked, with as much calm and quiet dignity I could muster.

"We wouldn't have to set it right away. We could set it out to before Christmas. That would give you time to plan and get used to the idea?"

Simmering anger and I'll admit it, hurt, swirled in my belly. I turned to Derek and asked, "You're okay with this?"

He nodded once and said, "I am."

All this time I'd been spending with my family and Derek, I thought they were seeing me as more than just a wolf's mate. I thought I was showing them I was worth more than just as a breeder. I wanted to go to school and have a career. I had plans. They didn't care about my plans and my wants. They only cared about their own. Fine. "I would be able to pick who my mate would be?"

Derek almost preened at that. He stood up taller, puffed out his chest, and a small grin appeared on his face. Oh, he was in for the shock of his life then.

"Of course," my grandfather said.

I stepped closer to Derek and a smile of my own spread over my face. I don't know if it showed the rage I was feeling, but Derek noticed something was off. "Uh,"

"Fine," I said. "I will agree to your terms."

"Wonderful. See, Derek, she took it better than we expected. We explained the situation and she could see the rightness of it. When shall we schedule the big event?"

"I think you are getting a little ahead of yourself. Shouldn't we first discuss who the groom will be?"

"Well, yes. I assumed," my grandfather began.

"You assumed incorrectly," I said cutting him off. My smile changed to a sneer

"I won't spend my life, what's left of it, tied to someone who would go behind my back, knowing the plans I have for my life. Knowing what I want and how I want a future to be, and gang up on me with my family to force me into a marriage you know I do not consent to, but am being forced into. Well, fine. You all win, but I don't choose you, Derek. Oh no. You don't get to win. You lose. I will formally mate, and I will do so before Christmas, but no, it won't be you."

I pushed his shoulders to make my point, then I turned to face my grandfather. His face was more than wary; it also had a tinge of uncertainty and a smidge of fear to it. Well, good. That was my life the last few years. I'd lived in constant fear of what they would do to me next. It was my turn.

"Abigail," my grandfather said in warning.

He didn't have a clue what I was going to say; he only knew it was not going to be good.

"Abby, don't," Derek said.

Maybe he had an inkling of where I was going.

I didn't stop to think about what I was doing. "I won't be mating with Derek. I will choose Brinn."

"The hell you are!" Derek roared.

To say pandemonium set it, would be an understatement. He stalked right up to me, grabbed my shoulders and shook me hard. "You will accept me as your mate, and it will be done immediately."

"No," I said calmly but firmly. I had to be in control, where Derek was not. "Gpa said I got to choose. That was the bargain."

"Derek, let her go," my grandfather said.

I hadn't seen him get up and I hadn't seen him step directly next to us either, but there he was all the same.

"She can't do this!" Derek was still roaring, but he was in a teeny bit more control of his anger.

"She can," I said, with as much snide distain as I could garner.

"When we talked, we discussed the danger she was to herself and others when in heat. The best thing for Abigail is to be mated. It will keep her safer."

I smiled a big toothy grin at Derek.

"Yes, we assumed she would choose you, but she did not. I don't know why she didn't, but she didn't," he continued.

"No, she didn't" I said, just to drive the knife in a little bit farther.

"It's out of spite," Derek said.

"Of course, it is." My grandfather turned a hard stare upon me then.

"You can't let her do this."

"We made a bargain. She will be mated and married before Christmas. You have six months to change her mind. If you want her, it's up to you to get her."

"I'm not a sweater," I snapped. "I get a say in my life. I'll be eighteen in a few weeks. I'm an adult and get a say."

My grandfather snapped his head and eyes directly on me, then said, with anger of his own, "Then act like it." He then turned and walked out of the room.

Derek didn't wait even a second before he pounced. He leapt at me, grabbed me by my shoulders and shoved me back until my back was against the corner of the room. "Don't play with me, Abby," he snarled. "You are mine. I will not have it. Do you hear me?" He pressed hard against my shoulders enough that I could say it was painful.

I began to struggle. I wasn't entirely afraid of Derek anymore. He was all bark and no bite most of the time. Well, usually when it came to me anyway, he was. Right then, though, I wasn't completely sure. I refused to give in. I stomped on his foot and shoved him back right in the chest.

"Damnit, Abby!" he said and hopped up on one foot momentarily. He didn't release me though.

"You don't get to order me around," I said. "You heard my grandfather. I get to choose who."

"Why are you doing this? We are suited for one another. I have feelings for you and you do toward me. Why, Abby?"

"Really? I have told you and told you I have plans for my life. I will not be mated off at eighteen years old. I want to go to college. I want to major in the animal sciences. I want to learn about humans and animals so I can help our kind. No one is going to stop me. Not you, or my grandfather, and not my father. I'm done trying to be nice and play along. I will have a life outside of this…this clan."

"I understand your dreams. I'd let you go to college and do all the things you think you want…" he tapered off there. I think he knew he'd made a huge misstep.

"Let me? You'd let me?" I growled. I tried to hold onto my temper, but I could feel myself losing control.

"That's not what I meant," he said.

I felt his hands retighten on my arms. He was preparing for my temper to explode. He wasn't a dummy. No, not really, but even he had to have known that holding onto me when I lost control to my anger was stupid.

"It's what you said," I spat between harshly clenched teeth.

I could feel the wolf trying to come. I was going to let it too, but I wanted to say something to Derek first, before I tore his face off. "That, right there, is why I don't want to be mated to anyone in the clan, you included. The fact that you think you can give me permission to do anything says how little freedom I would have. I may have to get married, but I'm going to make everyone just as miserable with this decree as I will be. I refuse to suffer alone. I'll take you all down with me. Now let go of me."

"No. We are going to work this out. That's what adults do."

I growled low in my chest and stared hard at him. My teeth were starting to push forward, and my face began to elongate.

"Abby, we need to talk this out."

"I told you to let me go." Those were the last words I could say as the change took over.

I felt what was left of my clothes slide down to the floor as I shifted, fast. I used the momentum to my advantage. As I felt Derek's hands lose their grip on my shifting and changing shoulder structure, I threw myself at his chest. I used my back feet and legs to push off the wall behind me and I shoved.

Derek lost his balance all the while trying to retain his hold on me. That was a mistake he probably wouldn't make again with me. He fell to the ground, where he landed with a hard thud, flat on his back. I felt the air push and rush from his chest, as I followed along for the fall, and hit his chest with the full weight of a grown female wolf.

While I was a little off balance myself, he reached around my neck and grabbed me by the loose skin and held on. He tried to pull me down to his chest. I couldn't let him gain that advantage over me. If he could get both arms wrapped around me, I would be in trouble. Even though I didn't want to really hurt him, I also felt out of control.

I growled as a warning. Derek didn't listen or didn't want to. I snapped my teeth in his face, but that did no good either. We were struggling in a serious battle for dominance. I was not going to lose. I was not going to allow him to dominate me. No, not now. Not ever. I finally attacked. The warnings weren't being listened to, so I camped my teeth around the meat of his shoulder and used my strong jaw to push my teeth down and break through his shirt and then pop through his skin.

Warm, salty liquid hit my tongue and I saw red.

In the red haze of blood lust, there was no fear. There was no pain. There was nothing but a need for more. I'm not proud of myself, but I won't take all the blame for what happened next.

I woke up from the fog of the blood lust, to being smothered and almost strangled by my grandfather and my father. I was flat out on my stomach. My legs were trapped up under me and I was snapping and snarling and lunging at Derek. My father was sprawled over my backend and legs and my grandfather sat on my back with his arms around my neck, pulling me backward and choking the breath right out of me.

I stopped mid-lunge and snapped my blood-covered mouth shut. My grandfather must have felt the change in me as he immediately loosened his hold around my throat. "We have her. Take a breath, everyone," he said. Although he let off a bit on my neck, he didn't get off me. My father didn't release his hold around my back hips or even take some of his weight of me either.

I looked in front of me and saw Derek. His eyes were hard, and he was mad. He pressed a wad of what was left of my clothes against his shoulder and I could see blood trickling down even with the make shift bandage. His neck had a harsh bite mark that went from the side of his throat almost all the way around to the other side. His arms were scratched red in some places and bloody in others.

I felt myself wilt under my family's weight, as well as their disappointment. It was heavy in the room, not just physically on my person.

"Derek, go on upstairs. I'll call one of our doctors to come take a look at your shoulder," my grandfather said.

His eyes met mine. I couldn't read them. I couldn't tell what he was thinking or feeling. All I could see was the rage. He didn't take his eyes off me as he stood. He didn't say one single word as he left the room. My eyes watched him the whole time. His shoulders were stiff. His back was straight. His footsteps, although heavy, were steady. He didn't look back at me and he didn't say a single word.

"Adam. Let's see how she is. Get up off her slow and easy. I don't want her to attack us." My grandfather gave the order, and my father did exactly that. I felt his weight slowly lift off the back half of my body. I didn't move a muscle.

My grandfather stayed seated on me, as if I was a wild mustang ready to bolt. He had no idea how accurate that was. My father stepped around so I could see his face and he could see mine. "Yeah, she's back. There's awareness in her eyes now."

I could see he also had a good deal of hard red and open scratches on his arms. His button-down white shirt had a rip from the collar down to the waistband of his dress pants. He must have come from work. I hadn't heard him arrive or even known he was there.

"This is the kind of behavior we need to put a stop to. I've let you run wild long enough. This is unacceptable. You could have killed him. Is that what you wanted? I don't know what is wrong with you, but I've had enough. This is going to stop. You are going to be officially mated and married and settled. That's it!" He punctuated his words with harsh arm and hand movements. As if the words alone weren't enough.

"Adam, now is not the moment. She's had a hard time of it." My grandfather was standing up for me.

I loved that man. So much.

"Don't," my father snapped. "I've let you have your way and allowed her to stay here with you and look at what has happened. She's out of control."

"All wolves are at her age," my grandfather said calmly as he continued to sit where he was seemingly unconcerned.

I didn't move a muscle though. I was not sure what to expect of the two men. My father was usually a little reverent to my grandfather, who was usually a bit aggressive and direct with my father. The current by-play was weird. Off.

"She's a girl. They don't act like that."

"Exactly how many full shifter females have you been around when they were Abigail's age? Oh, that's right. Zero."

Ah, there was the tone and aggression I was expecting from my grandfather. I felt his weight shift, but he didn't get off me.

"We have enough hormones and tempers flying around this house tonight, Adam, we don't need more from a grown man. You will pull yourself together."

My father's face was a study of emotions. Hurt, anger, and maybe a bit of annoyance. "I meant what I said. She's my daughter, and I will be obeyed in this. December first is the due date on this sham of a mating and a marriage. I don't care who she picks, but it will be done by December first."

He then turned his hard eyes directly onto me and said. "You hear me? I don't care if I have to drag you down the aisle, you will be married before the end of this year."

"She's already agreed to the stipulation, Adam," my grandfather said, as he finally stood up and I was free.

I didn't wait around to see what else would happen, I simply bolted up the back stairs. I hadn't made it safe to my room before my father's roar reached my ears. I pushed my door closed on the knowledge he'd just heard the second part of my bargain with my grandfather, and he was not pleased.

I quickly shifted and locked the door. I then ran to throw on some clothes as I knew the fight wasn't over and I was about to get another earful. I sat on the bed and waited, but he didn't come. I waited another several minutes and no matter how hard I tried to listen, all I could hear was silence. That wasn't a good sign.

I scooted backward on the bed, until I was sitting with my back against the headboard. I pulled my legs in and my knees against my chest. Nope, it hadn't been a good day.

Chapter Eight

I watched the sun rise on the following day from my sill of my window. I hadn't slept well. In fact, I had hardly slept at all. Most nights when I'd had problems like that I would have gone up to Derek's room. He would have let me in his bed to sleep next to him. I would have felt safe and maybe a little loved. I would have been able to finally sleep. I'd been afraid of the reception I'd get, so I stayed hiding in my room, unable to either sleep or go to him. I'd been trapped there with only my thoughts and those hadn't been so nice either.

I knew I'd let my anger get the best of me with the whole Brinn thing. I also was willing to admit to myself I wanted to hurt Derek like I was hurting. How dare he use my family against me to get his way. He knew how I felt about my freedom. He knew. I couldn't go back on my word now about Brinn, though. My pride was too much to allow it. What was I going to do?

I felt my eyes burn and my nose start to run, but I sniffed back the sad emotions. "Get it together," I whisper-yelled at myself. I'd set the course and I would head into the storm if I had to. They were not going to win. I may lose in the end, but so would everyone else.

I better go tell the lucky bridegroom the news. The question was how to find him. I got dressed and pulled my hair back into a long braid. I won't call it a tidy neat braid, my hair didn't work that way, but it was back and that was what I needed. I pulled on a pair of runners before I crept out of the house at just after the break of dawn. I hit the ground running and jogged my way to the forest.

I didn't stop once I reached the trees, I headed in at a trot, turned to the right, and kept right on running. I came to the area where I'd met Brinn the first time and I continued on. He may not have been where I hoped, but his scent was. I tuned in to my wolf senses and tried my luck of smelling my way to him.

I caught a fresh track which had his earthy smell. To most of us, saying someone smelled earthy sounded like they had BO, but that's not what it was with Brinn. It was almost like pine trees with a bit of fresh dirt mixed in. It wasn't a bad smell or off-putting; it was really the scent of the forest. It was a good clean smell. Which was good, especially if I planned on spending the rest of my life with the dude.

I rounded a giant pine tree, and almost ran right into my prey. Brinn caught me with a strong grip to my upper arms. I winced and jerked back, only then realizing Derek hadn't been the only one sporting signs of the fight last night. I had hand-shaped black and blue bruises around both my biceps. Great.

"Looking for someone?" he said, but he wasn't looking at my face. He was staring at my arms. "Those look deep."

I shook my head and said, "They aren't as bad as they look. I gave as good as I got, maybe a bit more than I got."

He didn't respond one way or another, instead he tilted his head and looked me over some more. He finally said, "I'm glad I ran into you. I wanted to say I was sorry about what happened. You know the last time I saw you."

"I remember," I replied.

"I've never been around a girl when she was like that. I couldn't stop myself and I couldn't control my wolf or even me. I don't know how to explain it, but I really am sorry. I'm not that type of guy. My mother would probably castrate me if she knew what happened."

I felt sorry for him. He sounded genuinely upset and sorry. "Look, it's not entirely your fault. Nature and hormones are not fair sometimes. I should be good for about six to eight months now so you should be cool as well if you are going to be around."

He hesitated then said, "What happens in six to eight months?"

I smiled a giant sarcastic smile and said in a sickly-sweet voice, "I get to go through it all over again. Isn't that great?"

"So, I get to be a raging animal with no self-control in six months?

What the hell is that?" He said it so incredulously and with such mortification I had to laugh.

"Yes," I said between laughter. "Being a shifter is not fair in some ways."

"Is there something you or I can do about it?" he asked.

I realized at that moment that I liked him. "You know what? You are the first male shifter who has asked what we can do. Not what I can do. Not what can be done to me. You asked what we can do." I shook my head at the world, myself and puberty.

I sat down in the dirt, pine needles all around me and started to cry. Life was not fair.

Brinn knelt down before me and looked up into my eyes. "I'm sorry. Whatever I said, I didn't mean to make you cry."

I laughed through a sob and said, "It's not you. It's just...everything."

He sat down next to me and didn't say anything. He only sat there quietly next to me. Waiting. "The wolf clans around here, they are not easy to be a part of," I said.

"How so?"

"Well, I don't know if you know this, but I am the first and pretty much the only female shifter in decades."

"I wondered about that. I've never been around one or heard of one, but I knew the moment I smelled you, you were like me," he said.

"Future tip, girls don't like to hear how they smell," I said as I wiped away the last bit of wetness from my face.

"Noted," he said.

"Anyway, from the moment the clans realized I could shift, and was a true female shifter, my life has been nothing but demands and orders and change and...complete dominance over my life. I wasn't born into this world. I was pushed and pulled and thrust into it when I was sixteen. It's not been easy."

"I know what you mean," he said.

"Did you know you were a shifter?" I asked.

"No," he said. "My mother and I were shocked and scared as all hell when I finally did. I'd been sick and weird feeling for a few weeks and then bam, full moon hit, and I shifted. My mother almost had a heart attack."

"I can imagine," I said and told him of my entry into the shifter world. "After my father knew I could shift, he tried to mate me off to Derek right then and there. I fought him tooth and nail over it.

"You don't like Derek?"

"At the time, I didn't. I hated him. He was bossy. He was mean. He was just so...demanding. Since then though, we've become friends. Maybe even, I don't know if you'd call it boyfriend/girlfriend, but we are...were definitely a thing. Now though they've ruined it all again."

"What happened?" he said and indicated my arms.

I rubbed my hands over the bruises as if I could wipe them away. "After the last week with what happened with you and how hard it was for Derek, my family went all caveman on me. They've decreed before my next heat, I will not only be mated formally, which between you and me, I don't know what that means, but I will also be married. They all just assumed it would be Derek. He was there all demanding it be him. I have until December first to be married, mated and settled." I dropped my head into my hands and just breathed.

"So, you and Derek are tying the wolf knot?" he said it with a tone of confusion, and I could understand why. It was very confusing.

I lifted my head and looked him in the eye and said, "Actually, no. To you."

He stared at me and I stared at him and then he started laughing. Full belly laughs. "You almost had me there. Hoo, you are funny. Man, if that's payback from before, you got me."

I crinkled my nose and said, "Well, it's not a joke."

He stopped mid laugh and said, "What?"

"You see, they were assuming and demanding. I got mad and I agreed to the marriage and mating, but I demanded I get to choose who it would be with. They all just expected it to be Derek, and truthfully had it been different it would have been, but not like that. Not being forced into it. Anyway, they readily agreed with smiles on their faces. Then I told them I would marry but it would be to you..."

He looked at me for a full minute then jumped to his feet and shouted, "Are you crazy?"

"Not usually."

"No. No way, we don't even know each other."

"Well, you have seen me naked," I said trying to lighten the mood. It didn't lighten.

"Not funny," he said and started pacing back and forth in front of me. "Why would you say that? Why would you bring me into it at all?"

"I didn't know you. I still don't know you. I just picked you because I knew it would annoy them the most. You are not from around here. They have no control over you. They can't tell you what to do, so if you don't agree, they can't make you. I will marry and mate, as that was the bargain I made, but if you don't agree, well, I get an out. I stuck to my part of the bargain. I can't be held responsible for you not going along with it. See? It's perfect."

"No, it's not."

"Why not?"

"What happens when you go into your...your...thing again? What happens when I get hit with the effects of it? What happens I can't help myself? What happens then?"

"Dude, I'm going to go through that for the rest of my reproductive life. You do know that, right? Every six to eight months for a long time, whether I'm mated or not."

He stopped and said, "So, why do you have to get married? If it's not going to change anything, what's the point?"

"I have no idea."

"I don't get it," he said.

I shrugged. "I don't either."

"Okay, well, what about Derek? Don't you like him?"

That made me sad to think about. "Yes, I do, but he took my life away from me with this plan of his. He knows my dreams and what I want with my life. It's not being someone's property and slave, having to do what they say without question. He actually said, don't worry Abby, I'll still let you have your dreams. Let me. He'd let me! Oh, I just can't do it, Brinn."

"Maybe you are taking it the wrong way," he said.

I shook my head. "I'm not. That's how they are. He really believes he gets to allow me to do this or that. My life would no longer be my own. It would be a never-ending fight for everything."

We sat there in the shade of the trees for a while. I was the one to break the silence and asked, "Can I ask you a personal question?"

He smiled and said, "Would it stop you if I said, no?"

"You are learning my ways already," I said. "Do you know who your father is?"

He shrugged and said, "I never really cared to know. Maybe when I was little, I wanted a father like everyone else, but the older I got, the more I didn't even think about it. If he wanted to be around, he would, right?"

"Yeah," I said. Then, "Did you mom ever remarry?"

"Nah, she was never into guys. Never even dated."

"That's a wolf thing you know," I said.

He swung around to look at me fully. "What's a wolf thing?"

"My mom was the same way. She never dated anyone either."

"Wait, but your dad is with her?" he said.

"Let me back up a bit," I said. I'd forgotten he didn't have all the backstory on my life like every other shifter I knew. "When my mom and dad were separated, for about sixteen years, she never dated, never even looked at anyone else. When I turned sixteen, and my dad came back into the picture, she picked up with him as if they'd never been apart. There is something with shifters. It's like once they fall for a wolf, they can't see another male. They never find love again. It's a pheromone thing or something. I don't have it. Males don't have any freaky control over me."

"So, because my mom had a one-night stand with some shifter guy, she has to be alone for the rest of her life?"

"Well, that's how it seems to be."

"That's a load of crap. How does some dude do that to a woman knowing what will happen to her?"

"If it makes you feel any better, I don't know if they realize it to that extent. They know they have some type of thing over human women, but I don't think they understand it's permanent. At least, I hope so."

I connected with his eyes and said, "So, how many women have you left alone and broken in your past?" I said it as a kind of a joke, but also as a wake-up call.

He looked like a bit of a player. He was really good looking, and he knew it. That built body and big white teeth. Oh yeah, he knew he was hot.

However, the horror in his eyes told me more than I wanted to know. It was a lot of girls and he was mortified over what that could mean for them and their future. "I didn't know that was a thing," he said in defense.

"Well, now you do. Maybe take a little more care with other women and their feelings. Just saying." I stood up, brushed the bottom of my shorts off and said, "Let's hope you didn't leave any little Brinns in your past as well."

"Oh my God, don't say that." He stood up too, his mind clearly not on me anymore.

He shoved his hands through his hair on the top of his head, leaving his previously styled hair in a wreck. I could almost see inside his brain scrolling through all the woman in his past. He looked a bit scared and I found it funny.

"I better head for home," I said. "I'm already in a bit of trouble with the family. I don't want to push my luck."

"I'll walk you back," he said and fell into step beside me.

"So, if you don't have a clan, how do you know about shifters and stuff?"

"I don't know all that much. After I shifted, I had this great sense of smell."

"Yeah, that's a bit disconcerting sometimes," I said.

"It's not too bad. One day I smelled something funny and I went to see what it was. Turned out to be another shifter. He'd never seen another shifter and I sure as heck hadn't either. He took me to meet his dad and they helped me to learn how to be a shifter."

Wait, his dad? "So, you *are* in a clan?"

"No," he said. "It's just me and my mom. Well, we are also friends with Martin and his mom and dad. They have helped me a lot. My mom, too. We felt pretty alone until we found them."

"Are they here with you, too?"

"Where? In town?"

"Yeah," I said.

"No, they didn't come with me. Martin is still young, and he didn't care about the hunt I was on. His dad just looked at me funny and said to be careful. He could smell the same scent, but it wasn't as…potent to him."

"So, he wasn't as drawn to me as you were. Maybe because he is mated?" I said.

"Maybe that's why they are so insistent on me being mated. Maybe my pheromones or my biology changes once I'm settled. How is that? What would change? Will it make a difference that I'm balanced? Geez, there are so many ifs. Who knows if being mated would even help me?"

"Balanced?"

I looked at him and realized something. "Man, you are so far out of it. Do you know anything about the curse and the gypsy?"

"Seriously," he said with such a look of disbelief that I almost felt sorry for him. Almost.

"Okay, here's the short form of our beginnings as shifters. A long, long, long time ago, a guy didn't like it that a woman didn't want to marry him, so he went to get a potion from a gypsy who was offended by him. She cursed him and turned him into a shifter. He did get married, had kids and time passed. There used to be boys and girls born to the families that were shifters, but as time passed less girls and less girls were born until there were none. Then there was me."

"That makes you a pretty big deal, then."

"Yep. It's been grand. Everyone bossing me about. Telling me who to be friends with. Who to marry, where I can and can't live, where I can and can't work. Oh yeah, it's awesome."

"Sounds like it."

"Anyway," I continued on with my story, "There was this big fight between the Grey family and my family, which are the two clans of shifters. The fighting began. I kind of got scared. I tried to make them stop. Somewhere in all the fighting I reached for my wolf at the same time she reached for me. We joined together to become one strong being instead of two separate ones. Before, there was the wolf. She was inside me, but separate, demanding to be let out and demanding to be in control. There was me, the human me. I was demanding to stay in control and keep the wolf hidden inside. When we joined, I felt us bind together and now it's just me. I am the wolf. I am the human. We work together and take care of each other. We are stronger together and we are both in control. We found a balance."

"So, what does balancing have to do with the gypsy?"

"When I balanced, I was pulled into another world or into a dream...thing."

"You were hallucinating?" he asked.

He looked at me from the side of his eyes as if afraid to face me head on.

"I'm not crazy, if that's what you are thinking."

"I never said that," he said.

"Whatever. Anyway...in the dream world, there was a young and beautiful gypsy woman who said I was the first to balance. The curse of the wolf was not a curse at all, but a gift. Once the wolves could find and understand the difference and were able to accept their wolf side, they also would balance, and the wolf world would finally align. Basically, they would be able to find happiness."

"So how many have balanced?" It was a natural question to ask, but I hated the answer.

"Two."

"Two? That's it?"

"Yeah, me and my aunt. That's it."

"Maybe the guys can't?" he said.

"That's what I thought too, but I know the gypsy said we all had to find our own path to it. I was thinking maybe since you weren't indoctrinated into the clan's ideology, you and your friends would have a better chance at it. I mean, it's all about acceptance of the wolf, right? What do you think of your wolf? Do you like him?"

"Do I...are you serious?" he said and stopped walking. I came to a halt alongside him and waited for him to continue. "The wolf is a nightmare. He's constantly fighting to get out and make me shift. It feels like he is tearing me apart from the inside. Yeah, I get to see better and hear better and smell everything, but it's not worth it. At all. Plus, now I find out I can't even date without ruining other girls' lives. It sucks."

"It can't be that bad," I said, as if I had any clue.

"My mom has had to move to keep me safe. Every full moon, I lose all control and the wolf takes over. If I could find a way to get rid of him, I would take it, in a heartbeat."

"Oh," I said.

There wasn't much else I could say to that. I hadn't been separated from my wolf side long at all. I hadn't had to fight her or struggle. It had been new and exciting. The full moon came the night I balanced, so I didn't even have to deal with that. I had no idea how it was for the boys. None.

"Well, then it's more important than ever to find a way to come together with your wolf. If you can do that, the full moon loses its power over you. There is no more fight for supremacy as you are one being, not two. You are in control."

"Great. How do I do it?" he said with a definite bite to his voice.

"I don't know," I said sheepishly.

"That's not much help to us, is it?" he said. He started walking again and I skipped to catch up.

"We can figure it out, Brinn. I know we can," I said.

"Really? How?"

"My aunt finally balanced, and she thought she never would either. She had been hiding her wolf from everyone, even the shifters. The only time she let her out was when she was forced to with the full moon. But when I was in danger, and I needed help, she reached for the wolf. She finally realized she needed it. The wolf loved me, as well, I think, and wanted to help. They each reached for the other at the same time and just like that," I snapped my fingers, "and she was balanced."

"That doesn't sound easy at all," he said.

"It doesn't sound it, but it can be. You can try. What's it hurt to try?" I said, trying so hard to make him understand.

We arrived back at the entrance from the woods to my backyard. I stood inside the shadows of the forest. I tried to think of a way to make him see. A way to make him try. "The gypsy said you would find happiness once you balanced. Don't you want to be happy?"

"Of course, I do," he snapped. Then he took a deep breath and let it out. "I'll think about it, okay?"

That was as good as I was going to get at the moment, but that didn't mean I was going to stop trying. "Okay," I said.

I turned to leave the forest and start for the house. I stopped and turned back around and said, "Wait! How do I find you?"

"I'm around."

"But, do you have a phone or something? Where do you live?"

He turned and headed back into the shadows of the forest. "I'm around, Abby."

I watched his back as he walked away, until it was out of sight. Partly because I didn't understand him and partly because I was putting off heading inside to what was waiting for me there.

I couldn't stay outside forever, though. I took a fortifying breath, turned and headed inside. Where there was no one waiting for me in the kitchen like they generally always did, which normally drove me nuts. For how much I hated being pounced on the moment I went inside, I had to admit it was better than the emptiness.

I made my way on silent feet to the library and peeked my head in. The room was dark and also empty. I looked at the stairs and decided to try Derek's room. I admit I went up on as quiet feet as I could. I didn't want to be expected. I wanted to be able to check out the situation before heading in.

I made it up to the third floor and there was movement behind Derek's door, which was shut to the hallway where I stood vacillating back and forth on what to do. Did I knock? Did I just stick my head in and say, "Hey?"

I took another breath and thought, now or never. I cracked open the door just enough to poke my head in. Derek sat in his window looking out toward the forest. Had he been watching me out there with Brinn? The though made my heart skip and my stomach turn over. "Hey," I said to the still room.

Derek didn't turn to look at me, but he did respond. "Hey," he said.

We were off to a great start. "I just wanted to make sure you were okay. I'm really sorry about what happened."

"It's fine," he replied, but he still wouldn't look at me.

"Derek," I said trying to get him to turn, but he didn't.

"What do you want, Abby?" he spoke to the window. His breath fogged up a tiny oblong circle when he spoke.

"Please look at me. I can't talk to you like this."

He waited just long enough to make me think he was going to ignore me. After what felt like forever, he finally turned to look me right in the eye. What I saw, almost broke my heart. There was such sadness and pain on his face. I knew I was the cause.

"How did it come to this?" I whispered. Even though I said it quietly, I knew he heard me.

"This is because of you, Abby."

I flinched back at his voice. Not so much the words, but the tone was so hard it cut into me.

"You are so proud and stubborn. You can't see anyone else but yourself and your own selfish wants."

I shook my head and stepped all the way into the room. "That's not true."

"Isn't it?" he still held my stare with his own dark eyes. "You heard I agreed to the marriage and that agreement made me the enemy. You didn't care what it did to me to sit aside and see you attacked, almost raped. I couldn't do anything about it because my own wolf wanted to do the exact same thing! You didn't care that all the males around you are struggling and in pain. You don't give a shit about any of us. All you care about is you and your dreams. Well, take your dreams and shove them up your ass. I have dreams, too. You just threw them on the ground and jumped on them gleefully."

"Derek," I implored. "That's not fair."

He turned back to the window and said, "I don't want to look at your right now. Get out."

"Please, Derek," I said. My heart was pounding, and my eyes were filling with tears.

"I mean it. Get out." He didn't turn back to face me. He just stared out the window.

I wanted to try to make him see my side, but I couldn't reach him like that. I left as quietly as I arrived. I went down one flight of stairs to my own rooms. I sat on the end of my bed and tried to get my scattered thoughts in order. Was he right? No. He couldn't be right. They were all out to control me and take away my freedom. Right?

I sat there a long time and went over the last few weeks. I had been focused on my own discomfort and no, I hadn't seen or wanted to see anyone else's. Had I been so focused on how unfair it was to be a girl and be pushed away from society and my family because they couldn't deal with it, that I hadn't been able to see the struggle, the pain they were in, trying to accommodate me?

Derek, fighting his wolf again and again to keep me safe, and all I could do was get mad at him for not seeing things my way.

"Oh, God," I said and started to cry. I covered my face with my hands as the realization I was exactly what Derek said I was, hit hard. He'd told me, again and again. He'd said he was struggling to be around me. His wolf was tearing him apart and all I did was get mad when he said he had to leave.

I crawled under the covers of my bed, so ashamed of myself. I'd been having a pity party while everyone around me fought and struggled with their wolves. How was I ever going to make it up to them?

There was one way, but at that moment, I wasn't even sure if Derek would have me now. I wouldn't even blame him. He'd been trying to tell me last night and I attacked him for it. How could I make it right?

Saying I was sorry wasn't going to be enough. I laid there a long time trying to find the right way to fix the mess I was in. Nothing came to me. When I could stand the silence no more, I stood up and decided I may as well go visit Sam. He was as alone as I was. He might be my only friend right then and the fact remained, he wasn't really even that. He was our prisoner. You couldn't exactly be friends with a jailer.

I left without running into anyone. I maybe should have left a note, but Tanner seemed to always tell everyone when I was there anyway, so they'd know one way or another.

I arrived at the little ranch house and went right in and down the stairs to Sam's room without even a hello to Tanner. I found him lying on the couch watching TV. I flopped down on the end of the futon by his feet and let out a deep sigh.

"Heard you got in trouble last night," he said.

I turned to look at him. His hair was getting long. It needed cut. His eyes were really blue today. Were they always that blue? "How'd you hear that?"

"Tanner is chatty," he said.

"Tanner," I said pointing up at the ceiling. "The guy never says more than two words to me. I wouldn't call him chatty."

"Yeah, well, he is, you have no idea. Since you've made him have real food for me, I had to eat with him, and he never shuts up, the whole time."

"Oh," I said. Then, "What did you hear? About me?"

"Only that you wigged out when Derek wanted to marry you and then you picked some stranger to be your groom. When Derek got pissed, you attacked him and tried to rip his throat out. I bet it was an awesome fight. Did you really try to kill him? Will it scar?"

Well, he had the gist of the situation if not the feelings that went with them. "No, he probably won't scar. Once you are fully changed into a shifter, you will find you heal really fast. I always did as a kid, but not like now. It's like, crazy fast. We have our own doctors because of it. We would be a bit of a freak show if we went to regular doctors where they saw that we healed in a matter of days for an injury that should take several weeks for regular people."

Since I was already in the corner with my life, Derek and my family, I figured now was as good a time as any to see what I could find out about Sam and his family.

"Sam," I said to get his full attention. "Can I ask you something?"

He shrugged and said, "I guess."

"Once you get to leave here, will you go back home?"

He went quiet and looked down at his hands instead of at me. Finally, he shrugged and said, "I guess. I don't really have anywhere else to go."

"What if you did? What if you could stay with the clan, or with me? Or even Tanner. You are used to him at least. If you had a place to stay, would you or would you still go home?"

"My mom…she probably misses me," he said.

"I'm sure she does," I said, but I didn't really believe it.

No one had been looking for him or his brother. I wasn't completely sure she even realized he was missing, but I wasn't about to tell him that.

"But, if I wanted to stay here, I could?" he asked finally looking me right in the eye.

"I would make sure of it. Even if I had to sneak you into my own house, I'd find a place for you to stay. I don't think it would come to that though. We take care of our own."

"How long will I be here?" he asked.

"I don't know. Are you doing okay here?"

"It's just boring."

"I'll see what I can do about that, okay?" I said and reached out the put my hand on his head. Then I jumped in the deep end and said, "I really am sorry about your brother."

"He was one of the only people who took care of me. He was a little…crazy and a little…different, but he cared about me. He was probably the only one. My mom, she was like my brother in some ways. She wasn't…normal."

"I think she had a bit of wolf in her, too. Like your brother, she had a bit of the wolf, but not enough to shift. I don't know how you got a full one in there, but you do. Maybe that piece of wolf made them a little different. Regardless, that has nothing to do with you. It's not your fault they were like they were."

I didn't know how they were exactly, but I did know how Connor had been and he had whack job written all over him. I can only imagine his mom was the same way.

Being poor isn't a crime and it doesn't mean you don't love your children, but I also saw him sitting all alone in the forest crying. He'd been dirty, hungry, and cold. Those things were not okay. The only one who came looking for him had been his whacko brother who then talked him into trying to kill me. I had all the proof I needed that the family was not a good place for one of our kind.

"Do you think if you went home, and they knew you were a shifter, one of us, you would be okay? Would they hurt you?"

"I wouldn't tell them. I would have to keep it a secret."

"Why?"

"They hate you...us."

He said it so easily, like it shouldn't matter that a group of people was so hated, that you couldn't tell them, your own family that you were one of them.

"You'd just keep it a secret from them? Forever? That sounds so sad. It is hard enough keeping your life, family and gifts a secret from the rest of the world. You should be able to tell your family anything. Right?"

"If they found out, I would lose them. They'd cut me out and probably add me to the hunted list." Sam's face showed the truth of his words.

"Wow," I said. "You think they'd come after you to...kill you?"

He shrugged, again as if it was no big deal. "It's what they do."

"Wait, you have a list?" I said realizing what he said.

"I don't, no, but the group does. It used to only have one or two names on it, now it was a full list. Your grandfather, your dad, Derek. The other clan, there's are a few on there, too. Some William dude is one of them and then I think his dad as well. You're on the list, too."

"Me?" I squeaked, as if I shouldn't have already realized it.

"Yeah, you can breed full wolves. So, you're dangerous."

Full wolves? Oooh, because the boys had to have children with a human, their children were half, but if I were to have children with a wolf, they'd be full. I got it. "It's not like I would even have that many children if I have any at all. I'm not about to repopulate the earth with my womb."

"Gross," he said and snarled up his lips to show how ick he really thought that was. It made me laugh.

"So, it's a hit list. They want the names on the list dead. Why the older ones? They aren't exactly doing anything anymore. Heck, most of the wolves don't do anything. They are just living their lives. Working, finding love, having children, paying taxes. What's the big deal?"

He didn't want to say. His look said it all. "Go ahead, you may as well tell me. Not much can surprise me anymore," I said.

"I think the word they use most often is abomination," he said.

He was direct...and brave, I'd give him that. "Yeah, I can see how they'd think that. What do you think about us? Do you think the same way?"

"Not really. I tried to. I know that is what they wanted. That was why Connor and me, we set you up so we could get you and kill you and be heroes to the family. Connor wanted that. Really bad. I kind of liked you, when you were a wolf. She was nice, and she was soft and warm. Yeah, I liked her."

"You do know she is actually me. She's not a different person or thing. I'm the wolf."

"I know, but she felt safe. I liked her," he said.

I figured it was too hard a concept to really explain to him at his age. He'd figure it out or he wouldn't. If he didn't find balance with the wolf, it would be a different being. So, what did I know? "Okay," I said.

"Can you bring her out? I don't mean right now, but can you sometime?"

It felt like he was asking to go on a play date with a dog. He really didn't get it. "I can do that. We will figure out a good time." I left it at that.

Now what? I needed to get him thinking about survival, I guess. Especially if he intended to go home and pretend he wasn't a shifter. "You know there is a place for you here in the clan? You would just have to, I don't know, become one of us and not one of them."

"But I am one of them too," he said with a bit of heat.

That was the first time I'd seen any emotion out of him since he'd been there. Finally.

"I know you are. I am one of the few people who knows how it feels to be tossed into a new and strange world, with the old one being shoved away and out of sight. All I can tell you, and I don't really know if it will even help, but it seemed easier to cut ties with the old world than to try to live in both. Things are too different and weird once you become a shifter. I should know. I lost a lot being a shifter. You still have time to figure it out, though. I don't know how long, but you have some time to think about what you want to do. It's not going to be easy either way."

"How is it hard? Can't you just not shift? That doesn't sound too hard to me."

Oh buddy. He had no idea what was coming. "Well for one, once you shift and hit puberty, the girls are going to be coming after you. I mean like stupid coming for you. The guys I know, who are my friends, said it's so bad, they stop going out into public places unless they have to. It's not something you can control either. It just happens. Plus, once the wolf comes out, he wants to always be out. It's tiring for boys. It's not something I have any perspective of, as I don't have that problem, but boys do. Sometimes they can't control the wolf, and they have to shift."

"Why?" he said.

His eyes were huge. He was listening and taking it all in. I hoped I wasn't scaring him, but I figured he needed to know, that he couldn't just go home and pretend nothing was changed. He would never be the same again.

"I think it has to do with emotions. When the guy and the wolf are mad, the wolf steps forward and wants out, or if he feels fear, sadness, I think it's the same thing. The wolf goes into protection mode, maybe?"

Sam was staring right at me, listening. Really listening to me. "Then there is the whole full moon thing."

"What full moon thing?"

I hesitated. What if he didn't stay? What if he took all this information home to the Hunterz? What if this was all just a trick to get our secrets? I guess it wouldn't matter in the long run. Once he shifted, he would figure out quick what the full moon did to the shifter. "Well, every full moon, the wolf gets to come out. Whether you want him to or not, he comes out for the moon."

"So, we are werewolves?" He said it so happily, it was hard not to laugh.

"No, we aren't werewolves. I think some of those stories are based off us, but no, we don't turn into half wolf/half human hybrids. We are either human or the wolf. Well, I guess that's not entirely true either. I can shift partly, but so far, I'm the only one who can. Others have their eyes go wolf or you can see their skin ripple with change, but that's about it. I have more control."

"Why can you do it and not the others?" he asked. "That doesn't sound fair."

I felt like I just had this discussion with Brinn. "Well, that's a long story, and one that will have to wait for another day. I better get home. I'm sure someone is wondering where I am."

"Stay. You can eat with us," Sam said.

His eyes were so hopeful. I admit the idea that someone actually might want me around, and which would also put off me having to go home, easily talked me into staying.

"You sure Tanner won't mind?" I said, as if that would even matter to me.

I wasn't there for Tanner. I was there for Sam. Trying to be his friend.

"Nah, he won't care," Sam said.

He yelled, and I mean, he yelled, at the top of his lungs, "Tanner! Abby is staying to eat!"

"Oh my God. Why did you do that?" I said laughing and uncovering my ears at the same time.

"How else is he going to hear me?" he said.

The door at the top of the steps opened and Tanner ducked his head down to see us. "Okay. Food in ten then."

He pulled his head back under the stairway. I saw his feet turn and head back up. That was interesting. "Do you do that all day?"

"Yep," he said. "It's actually kind of fun. It used to really annoy him, so it was even funner, but I still like to do it."

"Lord," I said, wondering if I should bring up the idea of an intercom for the house or if I should just leave it alone and let him have his screaming fun where he could get it.

When the meal was ready, Tanner came all the way down to say, "Food's ready."

We all filed up to the kitchen together and sat around a little round table meant for four. He pulled out a family-sized frozen dinner lasagna and set it, along with garlic toast, on the table, and we dug in. It was awesome.

"So, why can't Sam just stay up here with you?"

Tanner stopped mid shovel with his loaded-down fork halfway to his mouth, and his eyes lifted in my direction. "Um."

I swung my gaze over to Sam and said, "Sam isn't going to make a run for it. Are you?"

He shook his head and said, "Not now."

I turned a smile back to Tanner and said, "See? He kind of likes you for some odd reason. He wants to learn about the shifters and what to expect. Plus, he's a bit lonely down there all day by himself. Why can't he come up here and just be with you once in a while? I'm sure you both could use someone to talk to."

"Um," Tanner said again. Wow.

I turned to Sam and said, "I thought you said he was chatty."

"He is with me."

"It was just an idea, Tanner. Don't have a heart attack over it. However, you should think about how you would feel locked down there with no interaction all day and night. Just saying."

Tanner set his fork down on the plate and said after a bit more hesitation, "I will discuss the situation with the others."

"Great," I said. I then went back to eating. That was all I was asking for anyway.

After dinner, I couldn't put it off any longer. I had to go home.

Chapter Nine

The ride home was too quick. I wanted to make it last as long as I could, but even going under the speed limit, it took little time to get home. Urg. I sat in my car in the driveway and looked up at the house. It was lit up from top to bottom, all except for the windows that were mine. Those were still dark. After I talked myself out of siting there all night, I got out and walked inside, all the while expecting the inquisition to be waiting for me. I'd gotten a reprieve earlier, but there was no way I'd get out of it completely.

I opened the door to the kitchen and saw no one. The lights were on and the kitchen was tidy and clean. The only evidence someone had been there was the slight hint of cooked onion and broccoli still in the air.

"Hm," I said to the empty room. I walked further into the house and checked the library and it was also empty. I thought I could hear voices from the front room. I stopped in the hallway where I could hear, but not be seen.

They stopped talking the moment I stopped walking. "You may as well come in, Abigail," my grandfather said.

Oh right. Extra senses thanks to the wolf DNA. They either heard me, smelled me, or a bit of both.

"Hey," I said as I entered the front room, where my father and my grandfather sat talking. I looked around, expecting Derek to be there as well, but he wasn't.

"Where's Derek?" I asked.

"He needed some space," my grandfather said very diplomatically.

"He needed to get away from you for a while," my father interjected a bit more bluntly.

"Oh," I said and sat down in one of the chairs by the front window.

I didn't want to, but I decided I would try to hear what they had to say. I figured it would be an attack Abby discussion as it always was, but I was going to try to be an adult about it. I wasn't promising I would be able to, but I was going to give it a go.

"We, your father and I, would like to discuss last night," my grandfather said.

"Okay," I said trying to keep it simple.

"You and I came to a bargain, but we didn't discuss or think about the possible problems it may cause. Therefore, I would like to re-evaluate and negotiate a new one."

Wait, excuse me? I know I said I would try to hear them, but excuse me? I had so many things I wanted to say, instead I sat there starting at them, completely dumbfounded. I knew for a fact they would not have ever, never ever, renegotiated an agreement with me, had I made a mistake.

"We think it might be best to put some parameters into the possible groom."

My grandfather was trying so hard to be diplomatic. It wasn't helping. I was getting more and more mad the more he talked.

"You will choose from the clan," my father decreed.

My grandfather shot him a quelling look. Maybe it was his tone and demanding voice, or he knew anything that came from him, I tended to argue with just for the sake of arguing. This time I had a good reason though.

"No, thank you." I said it very sweetly. I had my anger in check, but barely.

"Abigail," my grandfather said, "we have to think of the greater good here. The clan will be affronted if we go outside it to another."

"The clan will be affronted about who I have sex with? I didn't know that was their business," I said in the same sweet tone, but there was a hard edge to it that neither of the two men should have missed.

I could tell my grandfather heard it, and I knew my father did as well, he simply didn't care for my tone. He stood and said in a harsh deep voice, "You will be respectful!"

I stood up and faced him and said, "Like you are? Do you think it's respectful for you to decide who I have sex with? Did you like it when the clan tried to do that to you and mom? That turned out really well for you, didn't it?"

"We should take a breath," my grandfather interjected.

"My answer is no. We can either toss out the entire bargain or it stays as it is. Period."

I then left the room without giving them any more of my time. I was holding onto my anger by a very thin string. One more word out of either of them, and I knew I would explode.

I stomped up the stairs all the way up to the third floor and stormed into Derek's rooms. Since I was already mad, now was as good a time as any to say a few things to him, too.

He was standing by the dresser, bare chested, a dark shirt in his hands. Was it going on or off? I shook my thoughts back to the current matter at hand. "I have something to say to you," I said and walked right up to him. I poked a finger into his chest. His hard, warm chest…

He didn't say anything, so I just went right ahead. "I am mad at you too, you know! You can be mad at me all you like, but I'm mad too. You turned me into a product, a thing. I am a person. I have feelings. I get a say in my life. Not you! Not them!" I swung around and pointed out the door.

"I know what you are," he said and stepped in closer to me.

I could feel warmth coming off his body. It soaked into my skin and muscles in waves.

"Do you? Then why would you even think to set me up like that, then get mad when I fight back? No. This is your doing. If you want to be mad at someone, go look in the mirror!"

"You're right," he said and wrapped one of those bare strong arms around my back and pulled me all the way against his body.

"I…I am?"

I was a little foggy there for a second. I leaned into his neck and drew in his smell. "God, you smell good." Did I say that out loud?

He grunted a quiet laugh. Oh God, I did.

He tilted my head up to meet his and said, "Kiss me."

"Okay," I said.

What was wrong with me? I was in the middle of a fight with him and there I was kissing him? He dropped his mouth to mind and connected us as if it were a first for him. He nibbled at my bottom lip. He tasted my tongue. My breath caught and I lost a good few minutes breathing him in.

Derek finally pulled back and said, "What are we going to do?"

I stared at him in utter confusion. "About what?"

"About you marrying Brinn."

"I don't know what I'm doing right now, Derek. I was mad. You and my grandfather, pushing for something I am not ready for. You know I don't want that yet."

"Why does now or later matter. Did you plan to be with me? Was I in your future?" He pulled me over to the bed and sat us both down on the edge.

"Yes. I saw a future with you, but not for at least 4 years. After college maybe. But not now. Not at eighteen years old. No."

"Why does the time or age matter? What does it change?"

"It just does."

"So, let me ask you again. What are we going to do?"

They made the mess of a bed I was in, but I jumped right in it and wallowed. I was just as bad as them. All temper and no brains. "I don't know."

"We need to figure it out. Together. Without anyone else having a say," he said.

The fact he said we needed to figure it out, made all the different to me in the world. "Okay," I said.

I remembered the last discussion I'd just had with my family. I may have already messed that up. If they would stop pushing my buttons...or if I would stop letting them. Ugh.

"If it helps, I don't think Brinn is all excited over the prospect," I said.

That made Derek smile. It lit up his face and his eyes. Why was he so attractive to me? "Well, that's good for me at least. Stupid of him, but works in my favor."

I wanted to stay right where I was, wrapped up in the warmth of Derek's arms, but I was exhausted. "I better head down. I didn't sleep worth a crap last night. I'm tired."

"Stay," he said and tightened his hold around me just enough for me to notice.

I wanted to stay. We'd shared a bed before, it shouldn't be a big deal, but something was changing in our relationship. I was realizing my attraction for him was heading toward the physical and I wasn't ready for that. Sharing a bed may not be a good idea, even though I wanted to. "I can't."

"You can."

"I want to, Derek. That's why I can't. I don't know that I will sleep any better up here than I did last night."

He tilted his head and asked, "Why?"

I was certain he knew what the issue was, he was just trying to get me to say it out loud. "I may be through my season, but something is different with me. I don't trust myself and I don't want to put you in the position of having to decide what I want physically versus what I am ready for emotionally. That's not fair to you."

"So, you do want me."

I slapped playfully at him. He was wiggling his eyebrows at me like a loon. I loved the playful side of Derek. The angry, dominant side of him was the problem. It clashed hard with my stubborn, proud side. "Stop it," I said on a laugh.

He let me slip out of his arms, but even letting me go, I could tell he didn't want to. "I'll see you in the morning," I said.

"Night." I could feel his eyes heavy on my back as they followed me out the door.

At least one person wasn't mad at me anymore. For the moment anyway. I had a feeling Derek and I would be clashing with each other until we were dead. Maybe that was a good thing. It would never be boring.

That didn't mean I wanted to be married at eighteen, though. I had to figure out a way to make my family compromise on the timing. There had to be a way.

Chapter Ten

I woke the next morning at just before noon. I must have been more tired than I realized. I rolled out of bed, showered, and went down to see if anyone was still even home. Derek and my grandfather were gone for the day, so it was pretty much me on my own. Well, except for the house staff.

When I'd first moved in, the guards, the cleaning people and the staff stepped all over my nerves. They seemed to be always underfoot, in my way and talking to me when I wanted to be alone. Now though we'd all gotten used to each other to the point we just went about our days by habit. A smile in passing was about it.

I sat at the little table in the kitchen, munching on a bagel and tried to think about my next step. I should probably go check on my mother. I hadn't seen her since our last discussion. The reality of the situation was finally hitting home for me.

She was not the same person she was before my father came back. We lost something, and it was not going to come back. I could either fight it, keep pressing the issue, and making myself miserable, or I could figure out a way to live with it. She had been honest with me that she remembered us but didn't feel the way she used to. I hadn't liked hearing it, but it was sinking in.

I had a home and Derek. I had my grandfather. My mom, my father, and the boys would always be my family, but that was probably going to be the extent of it. At least for now. Maybe my mother and I could form a new type of relationship. Something without all the anger and hurt attached.

I set down my bagel and knew that would not be enough for me. It would always hurt. It felt like my mother died and what I had now was just a replacement host. I needed to figure out how to move forward, though, without it stabbing me in the heart every time I saw her.

"Okay," I said and wadded up the rest of my bagel in my napkin. I tossed the trash and set out to the driveway. The first stop was to see my mother, make sure she was alive and well. Try to have a real conversation with her if possible, without holding the past over us. "I have to start somewhere."

I contemplated driving over, but maybe a run through the forest would do my mind some good. Give me time to think about what to say or do. I changed directions and headed toward the forest. I hit the tree line and began to jog.

The best thing about the forest running around the town was I could get most places from within the trees. Some were too long of a sprint if it was a time crunch but usually, I was happy to run if the weather was nice. In the winter, when the snow and ice and wind came, I let my wolf do the running. I loved to run in winter as a wolf. For whatever reason I didn't feel the cold. Hot humidity would still drain me out, but the cold, the wolf me loved it.

I hopped over a downed tree and took in the world around me. The scents of the forest had long since changed from spring new growth to summer green and growing. The dirt, while covered in debris, was dry, which caused little puffs of dust to appear under and around my feet as I ran. The animals were lazy in the warmth. There were no hurried movements above or around me. I could smell the animals in the forest, but they were sedate in the heat of the day. It was drier than it had been, but it was still hot. I loved that weather. The bright sun of the day pushed me on happily.

There was a stirring along my right which drew my attention. The smell said human, with a touch of wolf. It was also one I had smelled before, but at the moment I was unable to place it. Female…unkept and a bit ripe with body odor.

I slowed my pace, so I wouldn't be right up on her when our paths intersected. She came out of the shadows and I knew immediately who it was. It was Sam's mother. She looked ill. Had the appearance of half starved, dirty, and almost feral. She'd been a bit off the last time I'd seen her, but right then she was off her noodle. Her eyes were crazed, wide and red tinged. Fierce is what came to mind, along with the crazy.

Not sure what to expect, I prepared for a fight.

"It's you," she snarled.

Oh yeah, there was a bit of wolf in her. Not much, but enough to make the snarl more animal like than human.

"I'm sorry, but I don't know you," I said.

I didn't. Not really. I'd seen her, heard her voice, seen her place of residence, but I didn't know her. Had not ever spoken to her.

"Where are my boys?" she said and lunged at me.

I was somewhat prepared for the attack, but not for the ferocity of it. She was all swinging fists and kicking legs and biting teeth.

I dodged her arms, but her feet hit my shins and the muscle of my thigh, almost dropping me to the forest floor. I held my ground though and shot out a hard and swift closed-fist punch right to her nose.

She staggered back in shock. Good, maybe I stunned her into some semblance of reality. After no more than a second, she charged right back at me, so that would be a no. She hit out at me in a whirl of activity, so fast I was not able to block them all. She connected once with my cheek, which seriously made my eye feel like it was going to pop right out of my face. Then again, she caught me in the side of the head which made me see stars.

That was when I decided I needed to get serious. Before I'd been more defensive, just trying to not let her hurt me, but after the hard hit to my head, I was done playing. I punched back to her stomach, which made her huddle forward over her tummy, then using her own forward motion, I slammed her forehead down on my knee. That hurt more than I expected, but it was worth it to see her stagger backward, lose her balance and sit down with a thump with her own set of stars in her eyes.

"Stop it!" I shouted when she made to stand back up.

Her lips curled in a snarl, and her hands fumbled at her back at waist level. She pulled out what looked like a toy gun, but I knew it wasn't. It was real, even if it looked weird. She aimed it at my face. At the same time, I realized it was a dart gun, I jumped into action and slapped the gun away. She pulled the trigger. I heard the pop of sound and felt slight movement of my hair as the dart fly past my head. I pried the dart gun out of her hand and hit her over the head with it.

I'd seen that on TV and figured it would knock her out long enough for me to gather my wits and maybe some help. It didn't. In fact, all it did, was infuriate her. She leapt on me and it was an all-out brawl. She was growling and making this screaming noise in her throat. I was just trying to hold her off. Fighting angry people was one thing. Fighting angry crazy people was a whole other ball game.

I wanted to shift. She obviously already knew who and what I was. It wouldn't come as any shock to her. I was also stronger in the wolf form. I just didn't know if I wanted to hurt her that bad. If push came to shove and I did have to really attack her, the blood would make me a little crazy myself. So, I decided to hold off, but also to get fierce about the fight all the same.

I wrapped my arms and legs around her as I threw her to the side. Using that momentum, I rolled on top of her while she was still trying to get oriented. I grabbed her head and slammed it down on the ground. She was stunned, but not stopped. So, I did it again, and once again, until finally, her eyes rolled back in her head and her lids dropped down to finally close. Her body stopped fighting me. I stayed sitting on her chest with my hands on her head for another minute or two just to make sure she was really truly out.

When she still didn't move, I rolled off her and took stock of the situation. "What the hell was that?"

I was still panting myself at that point. It was more because of the adrenalin than anything else, but it definitely had me out of breath.

I looked around, because I had no idea what to do. Was she alone? Should I just leave and let her go? Did I call someone for help? I needed to decide quickly though as who knew how long she'd be out. I reached for my phone in my back pocket, and found it was not there.

Thinking it may have fallen out during the scuffle, I rummaged around in the fallen leaves, pine needles, and other crap on the floor looking for it. I saw the glint of metal out of the corner of my eye and turned to reach for my phone when a biting sting hit me in the butt.

"What the..." I spun around and tried to see what caused the sudden pain, and saw the glee-filled eyes of the woman, dart gun in hand, pointed right at me. I reached around and found the little feathered dart and pulled it from my skin. "Bitch," I whispered.

My brain went into overdrive. How long did I have before I went down? How far was I from home or from my parents? I didn't waste another moment, if it was as quick as the last time, I had minutes. I turned and I ran full out toward my parents' house. It was closer than home.

I could hear her laughter as it faded behind me as I ran. "You won't get far, little one. Run all you like. It will just make the tranquillizer hit faster."

I already knew that, but I had to get to the house as fast as I could. Darkness was already creeping in over my vision. My heart was beating so fast and so hard it felt like it was going to break out of my chest.

I could see the faded picket fence in the distance, and I tried to focus on the white of it. That was my goal. I had to get to the fence. That was safety.

My feet felt so heavy. I was slowing down with every step I took. The fence was in sight. One foot, one foot, I could make if I just kept moving. I reached for the little gate and tried to pull it open, but my arms felt like jelly. I couldn't get a good grip.

The fence was picketed but it was an old fence and the points were dulled with time. I simply leaned over the top, which hit just above my waist and allowed myself to fall over the wooden fence to land on the cool grass of my parents' backyard. I crawled forward to the two steps that led to the back porch.

I had barely touched the concrete of the first step when my body just gave out. The blackness closed in over my eyes. My last thought before I lost all consciousness was, I hope someone found me, before one of the Hunterz or the crazy lady did.

"Abigail?" a feminine voice said.

It wasn't Derek, or any of my friends. One, it was female, and two, they called me Abigail. I pried what felt like glue-encrusted eyes open and looked upon into the face of my mother. She looked like hell. She had dark circles under her eyes, and she had lost more weight. How you could be that pregnant and continue to lose weight was scary. She looked pale and old, but it was still her.

"Yeah," I croaked. Was that my voice?

"Your father is on his way."

I was so confused. "Why?" That was a bigger question than it seemed.

Why was I on the ground outside? Why was I at my parent's house? Why did I feel like I'd been run over by a truck? Lastly, why was my father coming?

"He'll be here soon."

That didn't answer even one of my questions, but maybe that was fine. I wasn't certain I could process anything at that moment. My brain was full of fog and didn't seem to want to work. I sat up and realized that was a mistake, a huge one. The world tilted and spun. I hurriedly turned to the side and threw up the entire contents of my stomach which seemed to consist of, bagel.

"Oh, God, I feel really bad," I said and flopped back down to lay on the ground. The world didn't spin as fast when I was prone on the ground at least.

"I'll get you some water. Stay here and stay still," my mother said and stood up a bit shakily on her feet. She was a bit unsteady herself and I realized right then she was really pregnant and really big. How far along was she? She told us at Christmas last year, so I guessed she was getting up there. I hadn't realized until then.

I don't take all the blame on that, though. She was always in bed and sick and I never saw her, so, it was just as much her as it was that I was oblivious on some things. I lay there on the hard ground and tried to regroup my thoughts. What happened?

I heard movement outside the fence on the driveway and my body tightened in fear. Who was it? That fear was what finally made all my thoughts align and I was able to remember the fight in the forest and the tranquilizer and my made and furious run to the house. I'd made it, just barely. How long had I been out? How long until my mother found me?

Oh, shit! My mom. She was in danger. I'd led them to her house. Did they know it was my parent's house? My brain, while sluggish a moment before, was now in overdrive and racing so fast with all the possible problems before me. I made myself sit up slowly, but I needed to look around. I needed to make sure I hadn't just brought a herd of Hunterz to their door. I couldn't protect my mom on my own. I felt myself start to sweat when I heard my mom start to shuffle back out the door. She came into view with a glass of water in hand.

"How long until he gets here?" I asked as I sipped on the water, my eyes darting left and right to make sure we weren't about to be overrun.

"Um...maybe a few minutes. He left right when I called and that was about fifteen or twenty minutes ago when I found you."

"What time is it?" I asked trying to appear unconcerned, but I was.

"It's almost three," she said.

Three! How long had I laid out there? I'd left the house at like one? I wasn't sure exactly, but it was almost three. That means I could have been out there for over an hour. I hauled myself unsteadily to my feet and handed the water glass back to my mom. "Maybe we should go inside," I said.

Her eyes were on the forest behind me, and I knew it may be too late. Her eyes widened, and the noise hit me at the same moment. I spun around and put my mother firmly behind me. She wasn't going to be any help with whatever was coming, but she could be a huge hindrance.

Coming from the shadows of the forest was the woman I'd already scuffled with once that day. She was charging ahead like a warrior marching right for us. She wasn't alone though: behind her and keeping pace were four or five, nope, six men. They weren't all that big in stature, but they were thick with strength.

"There she is," the woman yelled and began to run.

The men picked up the pace and ran behind her, keeping in formation.

I had literally moments to figure out what to do. I spun around and shoved my mother hard toward the door and said, "Get inside. Lock the door."

Hoping she did as I said, I turned to face the threat head on. This time though, I shifted. In the full light of day, without fear of what they would think or if anyone would see me, I shifted fast. I pulled forth the strength of the wolf, praying and hoping I could fight them off long enough for my mother to get to safety. That was all I was trying for. Time. Time for her to get inside and safe. Time for my father to get there to help. There were too many of them for me to fight and hope to win. I was simply fighting for time.

I saw a couple of the men flinch as they witnessed my shift, but they didn't stop their driving run toward me. Fine. If I was going to do this, I better just do it. I ran toward them as well. I leapt over the fence and tackled the woman mid fight. I was done playing her game. I was doing trying to be nice. I was so done.

I landed hard on her check. Her hair swung in my face at the sudden halt of her forward motion. I clamped my teeth and jaw around her neck and held on as we toppled to the ground. She tried to jab and punch into my body, but I wasn't letting go. I felt the small pop, when my teeth broke through the tender skin at her throat and I prepared for the rush, as the first drop of her blood hit my tongue.

It tasted sweet and salty at the same time and I craved it. Man, did I crave it. However, I didn't lose myself to the rush. That was a first. Not only did I not go crazy with blood lust, but instead, I became more focused. The red haze did come, but it only edged my vision instead of covering it and making me blind to it. Why? What was different?

I was struck from the side with a powerful blow. I shied away from the pain and saw that the men were on me. I couldn't let go of her throat though. Not yet. I had a decision to make then though. It would take only a moment to kill her, but if my goal was to leave her alive, which would take precious time to do. I wasn't exactly averse to killing, but I'd already taken Connor away from Sam, the idea of killing off his mother too, seemed like it would be too much for anyone to accept or even forgive.

I increased the pressure on her throat and prayed she blacked out sooner rather than later. I tried to ignore the heavy blows raining down on me. I was close to blacking out as well. I knew I had to do something and do it now.

I clamped my jaw deep into the muscles of her throat. I tasted the salty liquid as it filled my mouth. I yanked backward, hard. I felt the ripping of her throat as I tore it from the safety of her body. I stood up on her chest and turned toward the men who instinctively took a step back. They were smarter than I'd thought. I spat the tissue, the muscle, and the contents of my mouth at them. The hard mass bounced off one chest and fell to the ground. Everyone, me included stared at it for a moment as a puddle of dark red began to blossom under her body and inch its way toward the others.

Pandemonium broke out after that. The squeal of tires came loud and shocking from behind me. Not just one set, but two. A big gorgeous buff form came sprinting out of the forest and jumped into the melee. Derek and my father came bounding out of the two cars that came to a screeching halt in the driveway. Everyone jumped to the fight from there. Brinn stayed in his human form, and so did my father, but Derek shifted to wolf and leapt right in.

Derek didn't fight, though. I watched his sleek form push through the flying fists and kicking feet and head-butting skulls, to find me, where I lay on the ground among the feet of the combatants. I was exhausted, hurting and feeling pretty ill. Had there been anything solid left in my stomach I probably would have hurled again. Derek stepped over my body making a sort of bridge over me. He pushed bodies back, and people away with his head or paws. He was protecting me. Maybe another day I might have been offended. I was a warrior after all; I didn't need anyone to fight my battles. That day, I'd already fought enough. I didn't have anything left in me.

The drugs I'd been shot with were still in my system along with the blood of the woman. The human part of my brain saw the replay of my ripping her throat out and my body heaved and tossed up what was left in there, which to my horror, was in fact blood and water, and bits of flesh. I hurled again and again until all I was doing was dry heaving.

Wolf or not, strong independent woman or not, I was done for the day. I pulled myself away from the blood and vomit at my feet. Derek hovered over me. I couldn't even look up at him to tell him I was okay, but I could feel him dropping down closer over my body to protect me as he could.

The world started to swim before me. I was not passing out again. I closed my eyes and shut out the fight above me. I breathed in through my nose and out through my mouth. After a moment or two the world started to settle, and my heart began to slow.

I finally became more concerned with the fighting that was going on around me. It had pretty much dwindled down to a bit of dodging about.

The Hunterz, or at least that is what I thought they were, looked to be pretty much done. One of the big guys simply stopped and put out his hand and said, "Stop. This isn't getting us anywhere."

Brinn punched another of the men in the face, but it was more a slap than a real hard hit. He stepped back and took stock of the situation as well. "I could take you," he said, "but it's not much of a fight really."

My father stepped back as well. He was still dressed for work in his dress slacks and white striped button-down shirt. His black and white designer tie swung back and forth with his movements. "You are on my property. I could kill you all and no one would care."

"Wow, that's dark dude," another one said.

Had I been in human form or had the strength I would have laughed. He had no idea how much my father hated being called dude. It really rankled him.

"Fact, that's what that is," my father said in return.

"Adam," my mother yelled from the house. "Is everything alright?"

Aside from the dead lady sprawled out on the ground in her back yard, yeah, it was pretty much a done deal for the fight. "Stay inside. I'll be in, in a moment," my father shouted across the yard.

"Get off my property and don't come back," he said turning back to the Hunterz who stood in a group together over the dead.

I took stock of the situation. No one seemed all that hurt. A bloody nose here and there, but all in all I guessed the most anyone would suffer was soreness tomorrow with a black eye or busted lip, maybe a few bruised ribs and such. They'd all survive.

Out of the entire group of men, it seemed like the women did the most damage. The boys were playing at war, and the women were living it. I'd killed to protect my family. I looked up at Derek who protected me when I had been unable to. He still stood over me, taking it all in as well. Was he seeing what I was? I pushed my face against his neck and buried my nose in his dark fur.

I breathed him in and hoped he could tell this was my way of recognizing what he'd done and thanking him. I made to stand up and he stepped back to give me room. I took a few steps toward the forest then stopped and looked at Derek to see if he would follow. He did.

I walked with my head held high right past the group and the dead. I went straight into the forest with Derek at my back. He made one stop. When he was next to Brinn, he lifted a paw and placed it on his leg for a moment, then he trotted to catch up with me.

As wolves, together we headed home.

Chapter Eleven

There was a knock at my door the moment I had stepped out of the shower and dressed. "Yeah," I shouted.

Derek opened the door and poked his head in. "They want to see you," he said.

I didn't need to know who the 'they' was. "I'll be down in a few. I just need to dry my hair a bit, so it doesn't make a mess."

"Okay," he said, but he didn't leave. Instead he came in, took my hand, and towed me to the chair in the corner.

With gentle pressure, I let him push me down to sit. I watched him pick up my discarded towel and allowed him to take the brush out of my hand. "What…"

"Shh," he said. He began to slowly and meticulously brush the wild out of my hair. Since I'd been a child no one had brushed out my hair but me. It felt…weird and wonderful at the same time. He didn't say a word and I didn't say anything to break the spell. Once he had it in a semblance of order, he scrunched the ends up in the towel to soak up some of the wet. After he'd pulled what water he could from my mane of hair, he tossed the towel onto my bed, and squatted down in front of me. His eyes, dark and intense, held mine. I reached out and ran the pad of my finger down the curve of his jaw. It was prickly under my fingertip, like sandpaper. "You need to shave," I whispered.

"Yeah," he said.

He leaned in and captured my lips. It was a sweet kiss. Not rough and hot and full of raging out-of-control hormones. It was exactly what I needed, and he knew it. This Derek was what I wanted forever.

I pulled back and looked into his eyes. I realized I could handle all the hot emotion that came with Derek, as long as I also got to have this side of him as well. "Okay," I said.

He smiled. "Okay, what?" he replied.

"I'll choose you," I said.

"For what?"

I smiled then, as I knew he just wanted me to say it. Out loud. "I'll marry you, before December."

"You sure?"

I could have been sarcastic and made a joke about it, but this wasn't a joking matter. "Yes, I'm sure."

"Why now? Why not before?"

I shrugged but decided to be honest for once. "I felt cornered. I felt like you'd betrayed me and set me up. I figured if I had to be miserable for the rest of my life, I'd be sure to make everyone else just as miserable as me."

"I get it," he said. "I really do. You also need to understand I am not like the others. Maybe I was before, but you've changed, and I've changed. We've grown up a bit. I want you to do all the things you dream of. I want you to be happy. You know that, right?" he said.

That was probably the longest string of words he'd ever said to me. "I didn't, but I am beginning to."

"College and life and babies, we are in this for the long haul. We are going to fight," he went on.

"I have no doubt," I said.

We were too hardheaded, and I was too stubborn, and he was so masculine. We were definitely going to fight.

"You can't just go off the handle like that and make decisions without me. I don't just want a wife. I want a friend and a partner too. You are one of the few women that won't just do as I say because I said it. You and me, we can make something together."

I figured I had some mental barrier against his woo-woo wolfy mind control, because I was also a wolf. I was starting to feel a little bad for the human girls who fell for a wolf. Did they lose all autonomy? Thank goodness I didn't have that, at least.

A quick unwanted thought of my mother zipped through my head.

She didn't have the same luxury. I pushed thoughts of my mother out. I instead focused on Derek and our possible imminent future.

"I will try to tame the stubborn streak, but Derek, this is who I am. If I have to deal with your unwanted attributes, you have to deal with mine. All I can do is try."

"Same here," he said. He then stuck out his hand and held it before me.

"What?" I said staring at the hand.

"Let's shake on it," he said but there was a funny twinkle in his eye.

I was on my guard, but I took his hand into mine to give it a firm shake anyway. I should have known better. He encased my hand firmly in his, stood up and without giving me even a chance to fight back, tossed me over his shoulder, and hurried to the bed, where he tossed me on it with a bit of serious flailing on my part.

Before I could gain my balance, I saw him jump up and come flying over to bounce over me. He didn't land on me as he'd caught himself on his arms, but the fear of it had me squealing and flinching all the same. He was laughing which made me laugh as well. He was so happy at that moment.

After rubbing his prickly face on my neck, until through screams of laughter I demanded he stop, he said, "We should tell the others."

I didn't want to ruin the mood, but I also didn't want to share our news with them either. I wanted to hold it between the two of us for a little while. Savor the newness of it all. "Can we wait?"

He froze and turned hard eyes on me. "Why?"

I gave him a gentle smile. "Don't freak out. I like the idea of it being just us for a moment. It's our future. I want to enjoy it before they turn it into a circus of planning and demands and all that they like to do to take control. Can't we just keep it for a week or two?"

His face instantly softened after he realized I wasn't keeping it a secret for some horrible, nefarious reasons. "Okay, but I don't know if I can keep it a secret for long. I want to tell everyone you are mine."

"And you are mine as well," I broke in, needing to be just as possessive as he was being.

I liked the idea of knowing he would be mine and mine alone. I'd never had to share him, but just the idea of it sent my blood raging.

"We do have to go down, though. They want to find out what happened today and so do I," he said as he crawled back off the bed and stood up. He again held out his hand, but this time I didn't hesitate.

He helped me up and we stood facing one another for a moment. I was the first to smile and break the hold. "Come on, let's do this," I said and towed him behind me to the door. "Wonder how long it takes for me to get pissed."

"I say under five minutes, knowing you."

"I bet I can make it ten," I said.

His laughter boomed through the hallway. "We'll see."

As expected, my father and grandfather were there waiting, rather impatiently by the frowns they both carried. I wasn't sure I would make it the ten by the feel of the room. Derek must have thought the same thing, as he leaned in and whispered, "Starting now."

Before we could even reach our seats or even get all the way in the room my father demanded, "What happened today?"

I continued on into the room, found my comfy seat, then took a moment to sit down and get settled before I answered him. Finally, I started with my confrontation with the woman in the woods, explained who she was, and why she was on the hunt. I continued on to getting darted, which had Derek cursing loud and proud. I ended with waking up at the house, and where they came in. Before they could pepper me with questions though, I asked one of my own, "What happened after I left?"

"As you know, by the time we arrived there, the fight was pretty much over. It was more for show than anything once the woman was taken out," my father said.

"That's what it looked like to me too," Derek said. "I felt okay staying with Abby while you and Brinn took care of it. Seemed like you had it under control."

"After you and Derek headed out, we had a bit of a staring contest, before one of them finally stepped forward, and said Margaret, the dead woman, was one of the last fanatics in the group. They were supportive of her, because she was one of the last of the original family lines. Since her boys ran off, she was it."

"They think the boys ran away?" I interjected.

"Everyone thought the boys left of their own accord to get away from her. Apparently, she wasn't all that sane," my father said.

"I could have told you that. She didn't even look normal. There was something about her eyes. She was just off."

"Tom said that most of the fanatics disappeared over the last few years and those that were left were more of the thinking it was time to let it go."

"Oh, sure they are." I wasn't buying it.

Years of hate didn't just end with the snap of a neck.

"I have nothing to go on or any faith in what they said but he seemed tired of the feud. Said it was just something the older generation passed down to the new. They didn't have the feelings associated with it as the older ones had."

My grandfather hadn't said anything up to that point, so I directed my question to him, and asked, "What do you think, Gpa?"

He looked from my father to me and Derek. he said, "I think time will tell. I am tired of the feuds as well. With the Grays and the Hunterz. I'm ready to just be an old man and let the young take over. I want to believe them because of this."

"You aren't that old," I said.

Maybe he was. He never did tell me his age.

He smiled and said, "I'm older than you think, Abby girl."

He'd never called me that. I was always Abigail. Formal name. No endearments. Maybe he was more tired than I realized. My father had a queer look on his face. Maybe he was as confused as I was with his father. Maybe he realized how old his father was and saw the truth in his words. Either way I wasn't happy with it.

"Well, if the feud with the Grays is pretty much all for show at this point," I took a moment to look each of them in the eyes before I continued and said, "You can thank me for that. If the feud with the Hunterz is pretty much all a history lesson for them, I think the wolf clans are in a good place and you shouldn't have to work as hard."

"There are still lots of issues that need the guidance of the older generation," my father hurried to say.

"Yeah," I said in full agreement. I figured there really was.

The clan still hadn't found balance. We had the new knowledge of the wolves that were not in the safety of the clan but were instead being born outside in the world where our existence could be discovered. There was still the new issue of connecting outside women to the males without knowing they were doing it. How many women were out there pining away for the man they were connected to and the man didn't have a clue they'd even done it? Yes, there was still so much that needed handling. "We have lots of time and there are lots of shifters and family that are here to help. The older generation doesn't have to carry the load all on their own."

My grandfather gave me a very regal nod. Just one.

I didn't let him or my father off the hook quite so easy, "I've been saying for years now the clans need to be integrated. The information between the clans needs to be shared. We need to stop holding back information from the young ones and deciding what they need to know. They, we, need to know everything."

I would have continued, but Derek cut me off, "There is plenty of time to hash all that out. One thing at a time."

I didn't like being interrupted, but he was right. If I overloaded them, they wouldn't do crap. "Fine. But I'm not going to stop pestering everyone until I get my way."

"We have no doubt," my father said.

Was he joking with me? Wait, what just happened?

"Well, I better get home. You mother was worried about you."

"I doubt that," I said under my breath.

He turned a hard stare on me and said, "She cares about you, Abby, very much. She's just confused with all the newness of life and the baby and Toby. Give her time."

As I'd come to my own conclusions earlier in the day and decided to accept what relationship I could get with my mother, I didn't argue the point. Maybe he was right. I doubted it, but maybe I could work on a relationship from here on.

The past was over, and I couldn't get that mother back. I could accept it, but I wasn't going to fool myself anymore either and pretend things would ever be the same.

"We have time," I said. It was the only answer I could give him. I couldn't agree, but I was done fighting over it too.

After my father left, I asked one more question of my grandfather, "What about Brinn? We know he's one of us. He helped me and protected my mom from the Hunterz. What will happen with him? Can he join our clan?"

"That is a good question for the clan and frankly, the young man. Does he want to be part of our clan?"

I turned to Derek, and said, "Do you know?"

He shrugged and said, "He has a bit of animosity of his own toward the shifters. Although he pretends otherwise, he feels he was abandoned."

"You know he's not alone though. He has two other shifters with him."

"I'm aware," Derek said.

My grandfather has some questions of his own. "Do we know their names? The name of his mother? We can ask around, see if anyone remembers her. See if we can find what family he belongs to. What clan."

I swiveled my head to stare my grandfather down, "We are one clan, divided by two angry old men."

He smiled at me and said gently, "Maybe, but that isn't going to change today. Today we are two clans."

"Fine," I said and let it go.

He stepped over to me and pulled me to my feet. He then wrapped me in a fierce, tight hug. I was shocked to say the least. Had he not been holding on to me, I might have toppled right over. He let go and stepped back. "You did good today, Abigail. You stood up for yourself and protected your family. You made me proud."

My nose started to burn, and I sniffed hard to hold back any tears that wanted to come out. Man, I loved that man. He was old, gruff, and stuck in his ways, but I loved him all the same.

"I have been talking to your father and we have decided our bargain was not fair to you. It was selfish on our parts. We were trying to make our own lives easier by making you do something you obviously aren't ready for."

I looked at Derek. His face was stoic, as he knew as well as I did what was coming.

"The bargain is hereby void. You can marry who you want, when you want."

"Yes!" I said and did a little jump of excitement.

"Just don't torture us with too many seasons, if you don't mind. I'm old and can't take too much more of it."

I leaned in and kissed him on his cheek. "Well, no worries then," I said and glanced at Derek, who had an unsure look going on.

At least with me in his life, I figured he would never be bored, and he'd always have to stay tip-top on his feet. "Derek and I have come to our own understanding. I have agreed to be his mate, his partner, his friend, and...his wife. I would prefer a spring or summer wedding though, so you all will have to live through one more season at least."

"You should have told us while Adam was here," my grandfather said in a soft reprimand, but the twinkle in his eyes didn't fool me any. He was tickled pink over the announcement.

"I like you better," I said with a shrug of a shoulder and a sassy grin.

"Of course, you do," he replied in the same salty tone. He turned to Derek and said, "Congratulations, young man. You have a prize in her. I hope you know that."

"I do," he said solemnly. He wasn't taking it lightly, the praise from my grandfather.

"See that you do. I don't want to have to show you the same treatment that our Abigail showed young Sam's mother."

"Ew," I said.

The picture of Margaret as I'd last seen her with the damage I'd done, made my stomach do a swift leap. "I don't know if I will ever get over that. It was not my finest moment."

Derek turned to me and said, "Yes, it was. You were fierce and strong and made us all proud."

I was uncomfortable with the praise, so I let it go. "Okay, then."

"Let's call it a night then. You must be hungry."

About the Author

Courtney Rene lives in the State of Ohio with her husband and two children. She is a graduate and member of the Institute of Children's Literature. Her writings include magazine articles, short fiction stories, several anthologies, as well as her young adult novels which include: The Shadow Dancer and A Howl in the Night series; Feathers, and Cold, published through Rogue Phoenix Press. For a complete listing, visit www.ctnyrene.blogspot com or feel free to contact her at ctnyrene@aol.com.

Also by the Author
at
Rogue Phoenix Press

A Howl in the Night
Book One in the A Howl in the Night Series

Sweet Sixteen is supposed to be a turning point in your life. The world is before you in all its glory, just waiting for you to reach out and grab it. Right? For Abigail Staton no, not so much. Not only does she suddenly lose her best friend due to a fight, but suddenly her mother expects her to believe that the father, she has never met, is actually a werewolf. With that revelation, Abby is thrust into the world of two wolf clans who are not only fighting each other, but also fighting for Abby, one of the few females born to the shape-shifters. Her father is determined to pair Abby up with Derek, a very dominant and overwhelming shifter. Abby vehemently balks at this union to disastrous results. When war is declared between the two clans, Abby has to decide what side she is actually on.

Chapter One

The day started out as any other day. I woke up. I showered. I got dressed. Maybe I did take a little bit more care getting ready, but then, that day was special. It was my sixteenth birthday. I, Abigail Leigh Staton, Abby to my friends, had made it. Finally. As of that day, I was officially allowed to date, one on one, no group date required. Not that I had anyone I really wanted to date one on one with anyway, but hey, I was finally allowed to. Oh, and did I mention I was finally sixteen? It was supposed to be a fabulous day.

I bounced down the hallway to the kitchen, where I could almost always find my mom. She was there, of course.

"Happy birthday, baby," she said. She walked over and gave me a quick squeeze. I beamed a smile at her and squeezed her back.

"You hungry?" She asked.

"Yep." When wasn't I?

My mom has always been the mothering type. If I scraped my knee, I got a kiss and a cookie. If I had a cold, I got a kiss and ice cream. My mom was the best. She wasn't old and embarrassing like other moms either. She still looked young and had a vibrancy about her. She still wore her hair long and down to her shoulders. We both had the same sun bleached, softly wavy, brown hair except I wore mine longer, almost down to my waist. When I say it was pretty hair, I am not being conceited, it just was. The rest of me was, well, so, so.

My mom and I were both blue eyed and stood about five and a half feet tall. Not short, but I guess not tall either. I was just average. What I wouldn't have given to have gorgeous legs that went on for miles, but no, my legs were just average.

My mom had sad eyes, though. Not old eyes, but sad. Even when she laughed, the happiness never went all the way up to her eyes. Deep, dark, sad blue eyes. I always wondered what the cause was, but I never had the guts to ask. Little did I know I was about to find out. It only took sixteen years.

"So, what are your big plans for the day?" my mom asked.

I didn't have so much as big plans, but I did have plans. Brian, my best friend, who also happened to live next door, and I were going to see the new horror flick at the theater in town around four. After that, we were meeting up with a few friends for pizza then we were going to take it from there.

"I'm meeting Brian later; we're catching a movie and stuff." I was sixteen, I didn't figure I needed to account for every minute I would be gone anymore.

My mom turned and gave me the one raised eyebrow look.

I really tried not to squirm under the weight of it, but found myself blurting out anyway, "We may meet up with Jenna and Carter for pizza too."

She smirked at me, actually smirked. The mom look was lethal.

We both looked up in surprise at the sound of the doorbell.

"I'll get it," I said, figuring it was for me anyway. My mom didn't have friends that popped over like I did. When I opened the door, it was not to a friend or expected face. It was to a short, greasy haired, annoyed looking delivery guy. "Abigail Staton?" he asked.

"That's me," I said and forced a smile onto my lips.

"Sign," he said, as he shoved a clip-board and pen at me. I signed my name and handed it back, at the same time trying to take hold of the package he was holding out to me.

"Thanks," I said, taking my package and closing the door, not expecting any reply. He was weird. I took my package back into the kitchen and sat back down.

"Who's it from?" My mom asked. She set my plate of eggs, toast, and sausage down in front of me and picked up my box.

"I don't know. Eww, mom, you know I'm not eating that thing." I was talking about the sausage. I ate meat rarely. Oh, I would eat eggs, and drink milk, and I liked honey. I just didn't eat meat, unless I wanted too. It had nothing to do with it being animal flesh or anything like that. It sometimes seemed gross and greasy and well, animally. Bacon was my downfall, that and pepperoni. If the world didn't have those two things, I would have been a veggie eater in earnest.

My mom simply shrugged a shoulder at me and said, "Hey, I keep trying. You and your meat thing." She then returned to inspecting the box.

"Here," I said reaching for the box. It was a simple square, surprisingly heavy box wrapped in plain brown paper. It had no return address. I figured the best way to find out what it was, was to, hello, open the box.

Inside, underneath packing peanuts galore, was a simple envelope, which I set aside, and a tissue wrapped present. I carefully pulled out the gift and gently unwrapped it to find a gold globe music box. Inside the globe a little brown-haired girl, wearing a red cloak, knelt down next to a big black wolf, encircled by a dark forest. It was a scene from the story of *Little Red Riding Hood* and it was beautiful. The details were amazing. The leaves appeared to be individually made. The girl had big blue eyes and her expression was not of fear but of affection. The wolf was huge, shaggy, and not scary like I would have imagined. He stood almost protectively over the girl.

"Oh, it's lovely," I said. I wound up the key and let the music play. It was a hauntingly lovely tune, soft and sad. I heard my mother gasp behind me and I turned to look at her. Her face was pale white, and her eyes were huge. The coffee cup she was holding was clutched with white-knuckled hands close to her body.

"Do you know this song?" I asked her. I didn't understand the stark fear, or was it surprise, I saw on her face.

She shook her head slowly back and forth then turned away. She took a deep breath, placed her cup very gently in the sink then leaned over it for a moment. When the music ended, she took another breath and turned back to me.

"You okay?" I asked her.

She nodded her head again and said in a surprisingly somber tone, "Open the card."

I cocked my head at her, as I tried to get a feel for what was going on. Something was happening. I didn't need to be psychic to know it either. I could feel it, from the waves of anxiety coming off of my mom, as well as from the feelings of confusion I felt from the unknown box I held in my hand.

I picked up the plain white envelope and opened it to a pretty pastel pink card that said, "*To my Daughter, Happy Sweet 16,*" on the cover. On the inside was a simple birthday greeting, but signed in large masculine handwriting at the bottom, were the words, *Love, Daddy.*

"Mom?" To say I was confused and upset would have been the understatement of the year. I didn't have a dad. It had always been just my mom and me. I had asked once when I was little why everyone else had a daddy and I didn't. My mom had told me that I just didn't and I would understand when I was older.

Well, I was older and I still didn't understand. Then there was the gift, granted an expensive gift, from a man I didn't know I was supposed to know. Oh, and then there was the question of where the heck had he been all my life. If he thought that by sending me a gift out of the blue, he would make up for all my life without him, he was wrong.

My mom ran a hand down my head, petting me. That was so not good. She stopped doing that, years ago. She then turned away from me and walked out of the kitchen.

She was mumbling under her breath. All I could catch was, "Why now? After all this time, why now?"

Since I didn't have an answer to that question, I set the music box down in front of me and ate my breakfast. After I finished and cleaned up in the kitchen, I took the box to my room and placed it up on a bookshelf. It really was lovely.

~ * ~

"Happy Birthday, Abby dear. Go on up, Brian's in his room." Mrs. Dean, Brian's mom, never seemed to have a problem with letting me, a girl, bust in on her son in his room. I thought it was funny.

"Thanks, Mrs. Dean," I replied as I headed up. I had so much to tell him, and I so wanted his opinion on the whole dad issue.

Brian was primping in the mirror when I walked into his room. Brian is not your normal guy. His room is clean. Like freako clean. No dust, no clothes, no clutter. It seemed so unnatural. Now, Brian himself, he was the tall, dark, and handsome type. He had dreamy deep blue eyes and shiny short brown and black hair. His lips were always smiling, and he had straight white teeth, thanks to two years of braces.

Any chic would be lucky to have him. I kept looking for a girl for him, but he always found something wrong with each one of them. This one was too giggly, that one too tall, another one was too blond. Whatever. Since he was almost six foot four, I didn't understand the tall thing. He said he liked my height. I wasn't giving up though. I would find him the perfect girl. I was starting to run out of options though. Geez, was he ever picky.

"So, you will never guess the day I have already had," I said, flopping down on his perfectly made bed. I knew this irritated him because it put wrinkles in the comforter that he would have to fix before we left. It was fun annoying him.

"Can I talk with you first?" he said, coming over and sitting down on the bed next to me.

This should have tipped me off that something was wrong, all by itself, because of the wrinkle thing, but I just sat up and said, "Yeah, sure." My story could wait.

But then, he did the most unexpected thing. He grabbed my shoulders, pulled me close and planted a big wet, sloppy kiss on my open and stunned mouth. I shoved him back, and said, "Bri, what the..." but he clamped down on my mouth again, pushing me back down on the bed, his body trying to cover mine.

When I felt his tongue try to invade my mouth, I figured I had had enough, so I threw a punch into his gut and shoved him off of me. I stood up and towered over him as he lay gawking at me on the bed.

"Are you out of your mind!" I yelled at him. I swiped a hand over my mouth to wipe away the feel of him. He was my best friend since we were in diapers. He was the one I told all my troubles too. He was the one I could always count on for anything. You don't kiss your friends. You just don't.

"Abby, you must know that I love you," he said, as he slowly came to his feet in front of me, straightening his shirt.

"You can't be serious."

He took my cold hand into his and I could see it in his face, in his eyes, that he was perfectly serious. That couldn't be. How had I missed that?

"No, no," I protested. "You're, you're my best friend, just like a brother to me. You can't love me, Bri. You just have to stop it, right now. I mean it."

"I can't. I don't want too. I have been trying to tell you for months, but you seem intent on throwing other girls at me. You aren't hearing me. Well, now you have to. I love you, Abby. I'm saying it out loud. Right to your face, so you can't pretend anymore that you don't know." He pulled me to him and tried to kiss me again, as if to prove it to me, but I turned my face away from him.

"Cut it out!" I said. I put both my hands against his chest and pushed him back, hard. His legs came up against his bed, and I watched as he lost his balance and fell down onto it with a bounce. I looked into his eyes and his shocked face. I am sure my expression matched his. I couldn't think of anything else to say to him so I very calmly walked out of his room.

I headed back home, but instead of going in, I plopped down on the front step. The green outdoor carpet crinkled as I sat on it. Elbows on my knees, chin in my hand, I brooded there, unsure of what to do.

I felt betrayed and sad. Did I just lose my best friend? I still felt his hands on my arms and his lips on mine. Why did he have to go and do that? Why did he have to think he was in love with me? I felt my eyes begin to burn, but I swallowed back my tears. There was no use crying. It wouldn't solve anything.

The sun was bright on my face, so I closed my eyes and simply let the sun's warmth wash over me. When I felt better, I stood up, took a deep breath, put on a happy, although fake smile and went inside.

"Mom," I yelled into the house.

"Yeah," she yelled back from the depths of the house. I shook my head and headed in her direction, hunting her down in the laundry room.

"No movie?" she asked.

"Nah, we had a change in plans." That was what I would stick with anyway. She would have worried too much if I told her that Brian and I had a fight and she would have absolutely freaked out if I had told her what happened. So, a change in plans was my story.

Other Books by the Author
at
Rogue Phoenix Press

The Full Moon Rises
Book Two in the A Howl in the Night Series

Life as a shape shifter is not as easy as it would seem, especially not for Abigail Staton. Being a teenager and a shape shifter is even harder, not to mention being one of the last remaining females in the two competing wolf clans and the only girl in her new schools. Striving to find where she belongs, gets sidelined when an old threat to the wolves resurfaces. The clans are forced to come together in a semi-truce, and the already dominant males become even more controlling in trying to protect their own as well as their secret. Abby finds herself in the middle yet again, but this time, she will need both clans in order to survive.

Shadow Dancer
Book One in the Shadow Dancer Series

Sunny has a gift that she has no idea how to use, until she meets Leif, a boy from the kingdom of Acadia, on the other side of the shadows.

Leif teaches Sunny about Shadow Walkers and how to use her new found gifts. As they grow closer and their gifts grow stronger, a threat arrives. The Shadow Guard has been sent to bring Sunny back to Acadia, to determine if she is a threat to the king as the rightful ruler of Acadia.

As Leif and Sunny prepare to defend themselves, Sunny finds that Leif has also been sent to bring Sunny back to the kingdom but for very different reasons. As a battle for possession of Sunny wages, she is struggling to come to turns with her feelings of inadequacy regarding controlling her gifts as well as the hurt regarding the lies and deceit of everyone around her.

Shadow Warrior
Book Two in the Shadow Dancer Series

Sunny finally makes her first jump to the Kingdom of Acadia that is on the other side of the shadows, for what she hopes is a vacation. Only her vacation turns into quite an unwanted adventure. Aside from new and unexpected issues regarding her relationship with Leif, Sunny meets the rebel group, makes new friends, fights with controlling her powers, and finds herself neck deep within a county that is torn apart by two sides, each fighting for power. Acadia is not quite what she imagined. How is she, one young girl, supposed to unite the Kingdom as well as unseat a King to take her place as ruler of Acadia.

Shadow's End
Book Three in the Shadow Dancer Series

The adventure and the struggle continues for Sunny, as the fight for control of Acadia is near. Battle lines have been drawn, not just by King Gideon, but also by the rebels that were once Sunny's allies. Due to unexpected trips to the ice realm and the fire realm, new allies are found to help build the Army of the Sun. There are new worlds explored. New friends and new enemies made. Ready or not, Sunny must prepare for what is coming as well as decide where she belongs within it all. But…what about prom? What about Leif? What about home? How can she, just a seventeen year old girl, rule a whole world? She's not even sure if she can get through finals.

Shadow Fire
Book Four in the Shadow Dancer Series

No one really knows who Leif is. They know the man he portrays and the things he has done, both good and bad. He was a boy that came from nothing and grew into a man full of rage that almost killed the one person he set out to save. He roams the realms waiting for death. Waiting for an absolution that doesn't come. Then a rumor surfaces. A threat has been made against Sunny. Leif sets out to try to right the wrongs of his past. He sets out to do what he was meant to do from the beginning, save the queen. Can he do it alone or will he have to do the one thing that is hardest for him, which is: Ask for help.

Cold
Book One in The Elements Series

Four extraordinary teens, each with a corrupted gift from one of the four elements: Water, Earth, Wind, and Fire, come together to face a common threat. Their creators, scientists of a genetic engineering company, have been hunting for them since they were children. Each alone and on the run for years, they inexplicably find one another and decide not to hide any longer. Before they can face their creators, they have to learn to trust one another as well as who they are and what they can do.

Cold, is Nora's story. Water is destructive all by itself but turn water to ice and it can become even more deadly, especially in the hands of an angry young woman out to right a wrong.

Feathers
Book One in The Fallen One Series

Feathers, brings you into the world of fallen angels. Orphaned since birth, sixteen-year-old, Grace finds her teenage world crumbling around her. Her home is burned to the ground. Her foster siblings and housemother are killed. Her life falls apart and there is nothing she can do to stop it. Her dreams have become dimensions where she can be hunted and hurt. Words like fallen angels, halflings, and nephilim are tossed around without explanation. When Grace sprouts a pair of wings, things go from bad to worse, as the fallen angels believe she may be the key to them returning to the side of God, but only upon her eradication.

www.ingramcontent.com/pod-product-compliance
Lightning Source LLC
Chambersburg PA
CBHW070335130626
46556CB00007B/2872